THE END OF MISS KIND

DONALD RAWLEY

The End of Miss Kind

Flamingo
An Imprint of HarperCollins*Publishers*

Flamingo
An Imprint of HarperCollins*Publishers*
77–85 Fulham Palace Road,
Hammersmith, London W6 8JB

www.**fire**and**water**.com

Published by Flamingo 2000
1   3   5   7   9   8   6   4   2

A catalogue record for this book
is available from the British Library

ISBN 0 00 226145 6

Set in Berling Roman by
Rowland Phototypesetting Ltd,
Bury St Edmunds, Suffolk

Printed and bound in Great Britain by
Clays Ltd, St Ives plc

To Noah, Philip, and, of course, John.
For all their support!

Beauty is a simple passion
   but, oh my friends, in the end
      you will dance the fire dance in iron shoes.

ANNE SEXTON

⊙NE

THERE WAS A MURDER, a very quiet murder, at the Cloud
Nine apartments in Canoga Park. Screams at first, then a
sound of rolling, of furniture being broken, then nothing.
Even the screams were barely discernible, if noticed by
anyone at all, and they sounded more like the muffled,
tiny cries of pleasure an obese woman might make when
diving into an abyss of pineapple upside-down cake, in
her own bedroom, of course, alone. The rolling was odd,
but not unusual. In Los Angeles people roll around on
floors and desks and dining-room tables for no particular
reason. They jump off signs and buildings, they jump

into marine tank lagoons full of killer sharks, they leave their children at the side of the freeway, or in the center divider, and drive off to Las Vegas or Montana, anywhere but here, and it is no longer considered unusual because it has happened before, many times. Furniture broken? It happens all the time, sometimes you sit in a chair and the whole thing collapses. No cause for worry. These are only things that you *hear*, not that you see.

It, this murder, the void, a moment without sexual definition but containing a heartbeat and two personalities, occurred in the nicest apartment at the Cloud Nine. It was the three-bedroom, the only three-bedroom in the complex, with new Berber carpet, designer shutters and air conditioning.

There were no common walls; a plus. Its small entry courtyard had a wall lava fountain that still worked, wrought iron gates from Tijuana and bird of paradise bushes splayed out in magnificent disarray. This is the kind of cheap apartment people wish they could find after a divorce, the kind of apartments writers hide in when they can't get a sitcom sold.

2   The apartment, 15-F, was always occupied. It once

had, according to the leasing agent, a woman named Tiffany Schwartz as a tenant, who, in her early seventies, still wore go-go boots and mini-skirts; it also had a damn good kitchen and tons of shade.

That was how it was before and after the murder. There are places where things never change, and the Cloud Nine, like its neighbors, the Hawaiian Gardens and the El Toreador apartments, keeps a smooth veneer on the sins of its occupants. Today the rectangular pool is still painted black to save heating bills and it is surrounded by tiki torches and a holocaust of bamboo, growing everywhere it can, bursting through the edge of cement patios and prying up the tiny screens of bathroom windows. In a Santa Ana wind the bamboo rustles so much it sounds like the building is on fire.

Then, completing this long rectangle with a pool in the middle, are the apartments themselves, with macramé hanging houseplants in the windows, or frayed curtains always drawn with the glow of a table lamp warming their edges, or signs from the cranky tenants saying 'PLEASE DO NOT DISTURB' or 'BEWARE OF DOG'. As the Cloud Nine doesn't really allow large animals, just birds and very

3

small dogs or cats, one would not have to worry, or beware.

This is not a building where children grow up; rather, if they are seen splashing in the pool it is automatically assumed they are grandchildren, or nieces and nephews from 'up North', perhaps Portland or Olympia, Washington. Or Salt Lake City. Not Hollywood, ever.

The tenants of the Cloud Nine are sensible people with secrets and unsensible pasts, not unlike the unfortunate tenant of 15-F. Never too old, but certainly not young, these are people who are comfortable hidden away. Which I understand, even sympathize with.

My name is Samuel Johnson and I am the last white Anglo-Saxon Protestant in Hollywood. I am sure this is not entirely true, but I never see my own kind anymore. I have been hired by the producer Sol Seagull (not to be confused with the famous film financier, although I am positive Sol would enjoy being mistaken) to write a screenplay. After six months I am still writing, and I feel

I am almost at the end. The conclusion is not genre. The conclusion is two days away.

This screenplay concerns the killing of a woman who didn't mean anything to anyone. There is a world of people who don't rate and who won't be remembered, who fade into convenience, whose wealth and privacy becomes the merchandise of thrift stores. The tenant of 15-F.

This woman was murdered so savagely, I often have to sit in front of an open window when I write, or I will get the shakes, and I haven't had a drink, or a cigarette, in seven years. I have learnt how to count these years, how to keep perspective, tally, amass. Even the arguable loneliness of routine has a reason.

With my movie money I live in a small, 1960s tropical box on Mulholland Drive. I have two bedrooms painted in hibiscus pink and yellow, air conditioning, Spanish tiled floors, a pool and a terrace overlooking the San Fernando Valley, and a sign near the front gate that states my rental house is electronically guarded, although I still have not found any evidence of an alarm system.

I swim every day, in the morning, go down the hill for

research and errands, and write in the afternoon. Sometimes I go out at night, alone, to a movie, a nice Italian restaurant. Perhaps look for love. Sometimes I show up in very glamorous places with a group of very glamorous people. I'm always the first to leave.

As of this spring, I am completely alone. My childhood friends are gone, my lovers from my delirious twenties are all dead, my one ex-wife of fourteen years died of cervical cancer in Spain two years ago. My literary friends in Manhattan feel I have sold out, and won't speak to me, give me two years and I'll be running back, so they say. I keep these numbers memorized.

I have no family. Bisexual and gay men have to make their own family from whatever is left on the road out and hope it sticks. Nothing 'sticked' to me. My mother and father raise sheep fetuses in Ohio, and they don't want to know me. Surprisingly, since I have turned forty-four, I no longer want to know them, either. What a relief.

Here in Los Angeles you choose your own backdrop and lighting, as long as you've got the money to buy it.

A second best is being young, loose and gorgeous, and

the backdrops come to you, hopefully with two neatly folded hundred dollar bills, but then I think too much of addition and subtraction.

I wish I could fall in love again, scrub myself of this slime that drips from jacaranda trees and the mouths of strangers. I wish I could find a man, or a woman, whom I could love. But in Hollywood this is an impossibility. I can't see their eyes. They take their sunglasses off and turn away, towards a mirror or someone more important.

I find myself looking over my shoulder to see if I am being followed. It is a constant, odd sensation and it rattles me. Since I began this project I have received letters with no sentences, and there were scratches on my front door. I find myself expecting noises that don't belong in their time-frame, creaking gates, ringing telephones with no one at the other end of the line. I know I've sensed voices whispering in back of me at the Polo Lounge and the Luna Park Club. A breath on my back in one hundred degrees heat. I am frightened.

The only way I can discuss this murder is by writing it on the page as a story, with me in it, with everything in it I understand and have been made aware of.

The screenplay I have been hired to write on the murder is, of course, a complete fabrication. It has been stretched, jazzed up, toned down, made very accessible, I suppose. A lot of people will make money on this. I am included.

I know far more than is good for my continued health and happiness, and I am sure something bad is going to happen. Perhaps I have seen too many Hitchcock films. Perhaps my imagination is overworked and my senses are too alert. Paranoia is a new companion, albeit a faceless one.

I write movies and I still don't understand them. I am not sure at what point our souls are stolen; Indians in the Amazon shy away from cameras because they believe the soul becomes trapped on film. All I know is the end of the world is coming, through Hollywood. If you don't believe me, just watch for the decay. You can smell it. You'll be able to smell it on the moon.

I miss being loved. I do. There is no love here. There was never anything here. Of consequence, reality. And nothing here lasts.

8   Los Angeles should have stayed a migrant farm town

with orange trees and tomato fields. But instead the devil came up from his residence, spit a bit in the basin and said, 'This will become the Beverly Hills Hotel,' and laughed all the way back to hell.

I live in a city choking with ghosts and heavy perfume, tumbling towards the Pacific. If only there were volcanoes here, then things would make sense. Ghosts are everywhere, holding my hand. Ghosts are telling me not to expect a happy ending.

You see, I know life in the ruins is treacherous at best. And everyone here is slightly ruined; like a grease spot on an expensive, no, make that a ridiculously expensive, sweater.

Certain ancient temples in the Greek Islands are overrun with hungry, wild rats. Here in the Hollywood Hills, coyotes are still discovered in newborns' nurseries with blood on their chops and yellow eyes. The producer's wife, the movie star's wife, the studio head's wife, they all run out into the jasmine-scented night with a bloody child in their arms, screaming. When calm enough to speak, they repeat over and over, 'My husband is on location, my husband is on location.'

9

But coyotes are a big cliché in Los Angeles. As, I suppose, are screenwriters. There are just too damn many of us. We are not liked. Having proliferated beyond acceptance, coyotes, rattlesnakes and screenwriters are considered a public nuisance. Take a shovel or a gun, but get rid of us.

In the north of the San Fernando Valley, news cameras point to a cougar sitting on a tiled roof on a brand new Mediterranean 'villa', eating a small domestic dog. We are all running wild through tall grass and broken walls. And we are all hungry.

TWO⊙

TO CONTINUE, BACKTRACKING, ROLLING the film to its beginning. A child can now do this with a VCR and remote
control. A child can freeze frame, rewind, fast forward.
A child can eject, but in a movie theater, the lights have
to go down, and the film stops. Oh sure, there is the
comforting light emanating from the projectionist's
booth. We *know* he is there, backtracking. We know the
movie will start again, right away, and we pause in the
silence, in the dim dark blue lights on the wall, spaced
every ten aisles, in the darkness that has left us powerless.

It is here we suddenly ask questions. Well, why did

the hero jump out of the car before it flew off the cliff? No one even hinted in the film the car's brakes were shot. How were we supposed to know? And why wasn't he more bloody when he got up? He jumped out of an out-of-control car into sagebrush, rock and cacti. How can he walk? He only has a smudge on his cheek. Wouldn't his face be torn to shreds? We then accept the film for what it is, not what it should be. We decide it isn't important to know the small details; it's the grand gesture that counts, keeping us in our seats. If we knew too much, all the small details, we would fidget, eat too much popcorn, not enjoy ourselves, complain about the film afterwards.

At the Cloud Nine there was never any backtracking, no chance to sit in the darkness and disseminate. Like any entertainment that has no pretensions of being art, life at the Cloud Nine was lived in broad but simple gestures, without shading. There was no reason to ask why a door might have been unlocked, for a stranger or a secret lover, or why no one seemed to hear the muffled opera of death from 15-F. After all, the Cloud Nine was built in the late Forties, when walls were thick. And everyone minded their own business.

In 5-C, there was an actress, June Spring, first a starlet at Republic in the early Fifties, then a character woman in television and radio. June strangled a child when she was only a child herself. She was seven and the victim, her second cousin, Myron, was only four. It was at the once a year family barbecue in Garden City, New Jersey, sometime before the Second World War. Myron had made her so mad. She doesn't remember why, as it was a place far away. That was always June's version; long ago and far away, a torch song she sang in a B-picture with Rory Calhoun that went nowhere, and she remembers wearing a white satin strapless dress and a diamond butterfly in her hair. She broke down when the producer's son, a little boy just five years old, stepped out of the shadows and grinned at her. End of her career at Republic. When she mentioned this to me, her eyes glazed over as she played a Benny Goodman tape in a portable tapedeck by the pool.

She waves her hands in her gritty San Fernando Valley dusk, listening to the bamboo stirring and whispered, 'My punishment is living to be very, very old.' Yet June, although not too swift, seemed a thrifty lady and also a stable one; a settled, long-time resident of the Cloud Nine, June still had enough money for facelifts and a new Eldorado every three years.

'I never knew the girl,' June whispered. 'I knew she was in the business, but she wasn't talent, you know? Talent and the office people just don't socialize,' June stated sincerely. 'And besides, I had a day's work at Sony Pictures, all the way over in Culver City, next to my beloved MGM, and I didn't see anything, or hear anything.' For all actresses June's age, successful or not, MGM is 'beloved'. A 'never again in my time' kind of place.

'June Spring was paid off by a big politico,' announced Mr and Mrs Rotella in hushed compliance. The Rotellas were in 5-D, right below Miss Spring, and Elyse, Mrs Rotella, has told everyone in the complex about the tears and late-night, hysterical phone calls they've heard above them.

'And the walls are pretty thick,' noted Mr Rotella with a jab of his finger and a nod of his head. 'Built by veterans, this whole building. Not a screw loose. So if we can hear it, well, the old gal must get pretty loud.'

14

Although Mr Rotella, Hank to his friends, played golf twice a week and Elyse always bought the best cuts of beef at Hughes, I could smell the precise aroma of failure about the two. I had to explain to the Rotellas, as I did all the tenants, that a movie was going to be made on the end of Miss Kind, the victim of 15-F. Her full name: Miss Kathi Kind.

'If you put us in the picture you can use our names, but we'll want money,' snapped Elyse in a strangely cheerful manner.

'I need all the small details, things you might have passed over,' I said earnestly to the Rotellas, who stared at me blankly.

'The police have all the important stuff,' Hank said simply.

The Rotellas seemed oblivious of age, thin skin a pulsing pink, due to the constant inhalation of generic gin and days spent in air-conditioned senior citizen centers.

I found out all about the Rotellas and everyone else at the Cloud Nine because I sat for several weeks, in the San Fernando Valley twilights, with a tape recorder and liter bottles of expensive liquor (Dewar's and Boodles were Cloud Nine favorites), ice and mixes, just ready for a pleasant chat.

I found out that the actual managers of the Cloud Nine were an elderly gay couple named Herb and Matt, who remembered each tenant's birthday with a box of donuts and a dirty card. I knew that Louise Shearer and Martin Fogelson in 5-B were both bodybuilders who had begun to lose their muscle to beer and laziness, but still made quite an impression on the other tenants when they preened and stretched by the pool on weekday afternoons. 'When *normal* people are at work,' Mrs Rotella added cryptically.

Everyone loved to talk and drink, but no one knew anything about Kathi Kind. Everyone drank and sputtered through those dusks, but no one volunteered the small details, the things that don't make sense, those perfidy objects of irregularity you find in a movie theater, in the dark, when the backtracking is done.

'She was a nice, normal girl,' said Marlene Morley, an extra and hostess at Barone's Italian restaurant. So it was certainly a surprise to the tenants of Cloud Nine, who of course had seen Kathi Kind enter and leave the complex

16

in a nice, normal fashion, every day for many years. Normalcy was the Cloud Nine's pulse. Kathi was always respected because she kept 15-F in such lovely condition. A nod in passing, always a pleasant smile. So it was quite a shock to the inhabitants of the Cloud Nine that Miss Kind had her exit chosen for her in such a grisly fashion, and in the best apartment in the building, the apartment where nothing should ever happen.

What is of interest is that Kathi was discovered at eleven fifteen a.m.; by five that afternoon the body had already been delivered to the coroner, the apartment dusted for fingerprints, which weren't there, the quotas and paperwork done, and the yellow crime scene plastic tags taken down. It seemed so neat as to be horrific.

By seven that evening, the news wires had the information, and by ten p.m. Pacific Standard Time, the producer, Sol Seagull, had bought the rights to Kathi Kind's life, and death, from her sister Sue Ellen, a housewife in Phoenix, Arizona. And then Sol Seagull called me the same night, to come to LA to write the script.

17

Kathi Kind was discovered in the little third bedroom of her quiet apartment at the Cloud Nine on a Sunday morning, an unusually cool August day in Los Angeles. Her murder made three columns in the *Valley Metro* section of the *Los Angeles Times*.

Not only is the *Valley Metro* reality, but a slice of horror every day. Besides the obituaries for Van Nuys school teachers named Mary Ellen and Gloria Jean who die at ninety-eight and have well-attended funerals, there is other news: real estate scandals, wild animals in back yards, city planning bitchiness, but more than anything, the San Fernando Valley and neighborhoods north, up to Palmdale, is murder central.

Perhaps it is because of all of the bedrooms with locked doors, the orange and lemon trees in backyards rotting away in the heat, never watered; or the children kept in closets, the drugs on the coffee table, all those adult tapes from the local video store just waiting to be watched.

Perhaps it is because Forest Lawn Mortuaries, with its rolling lawns, Roman- and Greek-style buildings and guided tours, is just minutes away, with many locations to serve you. Or the fact that the wide flat desert streets have the names of Spanish saints and dead film stars. Take Van Nuys or Ventura or DeSoto or Sepulveda and you can just keep going and going, almost for ever. There are so many roads out it is easy to disappear. Who knows, you might wind up in Palm Springs, on Frank Sinatra Drive, wondering which turn-off was wrong. Or in the middle of the high desert, past Lancaster, the very last Los Angeles suburb. Here you might find a nudist colony, or a group of fancy bikers cooking up methamphetamine in an Airstream Trailer, or a dead baby buried in a plastic bag under a quartz rock.

Kathi Kind was destined to become a *Valley Metro* tale of the grotesque. The murderer, from what I can decipher, seriously organized the setting so that Kathi Kind would be discovered by the next morning, not unlike a studio technician doing preliminaries for the next day's shoot.

The Rotellas were passing by her front gate on their way to the late morning service at the Little Brown Church in Sherman Oaks. They had had a light, California breakfast, a half-grapefruit and two Cape Cods for Mrs Rotella, and a sausage and egg sandwich and two

Bloody Marys for Mr Rotella. After church they always went for a sandwich and more cocktails at O'Malley's Eight Ball, owned by Mr Rotella's golf buddy, Stan.

Mrs Rotella felt flushed and energetic in her new church suit, a pair of peach and burgundy slacks with a lace half-sleeve top, when she noticed Kathi Kind's door was open.

'Kathi's utility bill is going sky-high with that door open,' Elyse slurred pleasantly, and turned to her husband. 'You go and see what's going on.'

Mr Rotella, informing his wife they shouldn't pry, decided to follow her command when she arched a painted eyebrow.

He knocked on the front door and stood in the doorway, waiting for a response.

'Kathi? It's Hank Rotella. You left your door open, darlin'. You want me to close it?'

Silence. Mr Rotella could hear and see the air conditioner blowing, a new model with red neon plastic flags fluttering like fire.

'Kathi, honey?'

Mr Rotella mentally noted how nice Miss Kind's

furniture was, very sturdy, from Sears, in beige and sky-blue plaid. Hardly ever sat on, he thought. Not a glass out of place in Kathi's kitchen, where the refrigerator was decorated with thirty-six bunnies, birds, and hippos.

The only reason Elyse finally came into the apartment, as she stated to the police later over a jumbo gin and tonic, was that she heard her husband call out to her in a weak voice. Elyse prided herself on taking care of Hank's health. He never spoke in a weak voice. When she found him, he was kneeling in the hall in front of Kathi Kind's little bedroom. He was crying. His face and church suit were covered with vomit, and he had lost control of his bladder. He could only point. Mrs Rotella looked beyond her husband and began to scream.

The room stank of Chantilly and other drug store colognes, which had all been emptied over the corpse of Kathi Kind. Miss Kind's hands had been nailed through their palms to the wall, but they were not attached to her body. Nor was her head, which sat discreetly in her lap. Kathi's corpse was propped up on her grandmother's floral occasional chair, a teddy bear next to her severed head.

There were round burns on her breasts, still encased

21

in their lacy French push-up bra. Testing later proved these to be cigar, not cigarette, burns. The rest of Kathi's stuffed animals were placed around her, some in sexual positions. Her legs were spread, but her feet still touched the floor. What Mr Rotella finally mentioned to me, in the swirl of the sun's last rays, was that Kathi's face was turned towards her vagina, her nose brushing her own pubis.

'I have to forget, somehow,' Mr Rotella said as he spun the ice in his drink.

All blood in the room had been washed, very tidily, from the shag rug, the pink walls, and Miss Kind's severed corpse. All blood had been drained from Miss Kind's body, and placed in large white plastic paint pails, with handles and snap-on lids, which had been snapped on, so the room wouldn't smell bad when discovered.

In between the two nailed hands, one of them sporting a Band-Aid covering a wart Kathi had just had removed, was a photograph from the Forties, of a severed woman in a field, immediately recognizable as The Black Dahlia. No note was left; just the photograph.

*   *   *

Kathi was an average, nice gal. I say the word 'gal', because Kathi, who changed her name by going from a 'C' to a 'K' and a 'y' to an 'i', is, or I should say was, a true gal. Kathi was plain, fairly overweight, with no outstanding moments.

She was, however, a good worker. Kathi Kind understood the system. She had worked for the government, knew her paperwork, her computer, and all the other women for whom files and codes are the stuff of existence. These are the women who run the world. These are the women in slacks and nice two-inch heels, with big hips and small shoulders, who understand what the word 'perky' entails. Because somewhere in the shadows, when they were eleven and crying in front of their mirror, their mothers walked in and explained that they *were* lovely, inside. That their brightness and kind deeds would carry them through life, not their looks. Always be cheerful. Appreciate everything.

These are the women who have the right credit cards, memos, numbers, and never have a problem at banks. I hear them in line, then at the tellers' windows:

'Gee, didn't Tammy at the GSA call you about this?

23

It's just a deposit Al Com Inc, but we could do it with a postdate if the manager JoAnn's here. Hi, JoAnn, remember me?'

These women survive. Sometimes. They'll never be beautiful, and in their secret worlds they probably aren't very nice either. They eat alone, have a few friends at work, and they've never missed a day. Or got pregnant by the wrong man.

These women hear us when we whisper something awful to a friend. They are the spectres who loom through the windows of expensive cafés and count the number of beautiful women in the room. They live alone in those 'great deal' three-bedroom apartments, with a guest room done in pink. The little third bedroom is full of stuffed animals, and in a drawer in that little third bedroom, past the romantic novels and a bead hobby box, they keep a gun.

In their autumns, dusks, and sensible winters, they know of all things not meant for them, but for the beauties. Like a cancer, they think, these beauties are just tainted honey dripping from the hive.

These women have one pair of 'racy' underwear:

crotchless panties and a lacy French-cut brassière, which sometimes they try on in a half-light, posing from across the room and knowing that in the right light, the kind of light that surrounds Elizabeth Taylor and Marlene Dietrich, they too could make a man aware of them. Just three klieg lights away, they reason. Or two lit candles.

They take care of their aging, ill parents, sending them off to oblivion, a hanky and an alligator tear at the gate. They inherit. They invest on a modest scale. They take cruises, wear tight flowery dresses for ten days and nights, even makeup. They try to meet a man and fall in love. They consider hiring a gigolo, but don't. They stand in an ocean breeze, their vacation dresses in a polyester blend, rippling over their hips and thick thighs, and realize they don't have a drink in their hands, their necks are not covered with South Sea pearls, and their silhouettes mean nothing in the sunset. They fail, and begin to forget about love.

Facts are never deceptive. It is our initial reaction to the facts that shades us, delivering the ambiguity when we begin to question.

25

So the theater is still dark. The film has been back-tracked, because these are the small details we will never see. We keep asking questions. How long did it take to drain all the blood out of her body? Was a machine, or some sort of pump used? Why The Black Dahlia photograph? A copycat killer? Why was everything done with such care? Didn't anyone see a light? Didn't any noise alert a neighbor? It seems the only person who seemed to care about Kathi was her mutilator.

The next day my plane landed, and I heard on the rental car radio that a woman's severed arm had washed ashore on Santa Monica Bay, wearing a cocktail ring and bracelet, both in eighteen carat gold. I was not surprised. I only wanted to know if that cold, wrinkled hand had held a rose, a rolled-up hundred dollar bill full of cocaine, an antique compact, a razor, a gun, a railing to a boat. How did I decide there was cocaine and a red rose? Because in Hollywood, assumption passes for fact.

Above the photograph of The Black Dahlia, on a piece of Kathi Kind's personalized hippo stationery and tacked to the wall with a happy face, was a peach lipstick imprint, very Marilyn Monroe. When Miss Kind's head was examined, she was wearing peach lipstick. It was also concluded the weapon used to sever Miss Kind's head and hands was extremely sharp and fairly wide, as the hands were cut off with one stroke each and the head, approximately three.

Her lip imprints were an exact match. Which signifies before her death the stationery was kissed by her, willingly or not, or after her death her head was lifted up, her lips pushed together and pressed against the stationery on the wall.

There was no evidence of sexual contact, no hair fibers. No mistakes seem to have been made.

No one had been spotted with Kathi Kind for many months, but Kathi wasn't particularly a dater. At the beginning of the year, she had held a potluck dinner at her apartment for the girls at her Social Security office. The 'gals' included Alakisha, Rita, and Jody. Kathi also invited her Aunt Gretchen, a sixty-eight-year-old widow.

Gretchen had recently become a lingerie rep, selling at house parties, with a big pink suitcase full of bras, babydoll nighties, and peek-a-boos with names like 'Va-Voom', 'I'm The Boss', and 'Mistress of the Dark'.

When Kathi Kind was found by the Rotellas, she was wearing a 'Big Girl Va-Voom #2'. When Aunt Gretchen was questioned by a homicide detective, Mr Franklin Mangello, Gretchen noted Kathi only bought the 'Big Girl Va-Voom #2' to spur the other gals on, so she could realize her first commission. And, Gretchen noted, Kathi was sweet enough to pick the least popular color, a neon pink with purple lace flowers.

THREE

'DON'T YOU GET IT? It won't happen again,' Sol Seagull noted as I began delivering pages of the screenplay.

'What won't happen again?' I asked quietly.

'The murder, fool. The reason they never found The Black Dahlia killer is because he only did it once. This is the same thing. Don't you get it?'

'Yes. I get it.' I didn't sound convinced.

'Another thing. We got a great set-up here. Think Jack the Ripper, only real cool, hip LA. Or that flick with David Warner and Malcolm McDowell. What was it?'

'*Time After Time*,' I said. 29

'Great fucking celluloid. You gotta see it.'

'I have.'

'Remember how it moved? All the way, baby.'

'I'm sorry, Sol, I see this as a tragedy of sorts.'

'What do you mean, of sorts? Of course it's fuckin' tragic, Samuel. Back to that flick. You remember, Holmes is chasing Jack through time. And make the chick who gets it more sexy. Who cares about an overweight secretary?'

'She was an accountant,' I said sharply.

'A bean counter.'

I couldn't speak.

'Look, Sam . . .'

'Samuel.'

'Look, Sam, we're all sorry about her, you know. Hell of a way to go. But unless you can get Kathy Bates, we gotta go with something more sexy. And besides, we can't meet Kathy Bates' price.'

'Really?' I asked.

'Yes.' Sol sighed. 'I already checked.'

We are at lunch at Posto, the Italian restaurant on Ventura Boulevard. It is cool and thin and elegant. In fact, everything about this restaurant is thin. The lettuce and various Italian green were thin, but very crisp. The bread was hot and thin. My veal was sliced extremely thin, but big on the plate. I looked around, sipping a ginger ale through a very thin red straw. Thin women were fluttering to their tables in beige and taupe thin, thin cotton. I swallowed the wrong way and began to cough.

'I hear everyone from Miramax comes here,' Sol said in a low voice.

'Someone has to have made a mistake!' Sol whispered to me as he talked to his line producer on a cellular phone. We were in his rented silver Jaguar convertible. The top was down. He had run two red lights going up Beverly Glen.

'Are you talking to me?' I turned to him. My forehead felt burnt.

'Wait a minute. Tell the motherfucker to hold his horses.' He puts his cellular phone down.

'Goddamn film. Whoever heard of a film called *Femenina*? So as a favor to Chuck Tellers over at Disney

31

I *volunteered*, mind you, to produce it. It's a fucking bomb. Never again.'

He tuned the radio in to a soul music station. Marvin Gaye was singing, 'I Want You', and Sol cranked it up.

'This is more like it. The man was a fucking genius. Pussy killed him.' Sol laughed, looked at me.

I smiled. Driving through the canyon, I thought how Sol reminded me of Rod Steiger in *The Big Knife*. Sol had a hearing aid, cropped white hair, small feet in Italian beige loafers and a thick cock which he pushed over to one side of his slacks, letting it hang down his leg, unencumbered by underwear. Unfortunately, if Sol was twenty-five, this would be of interest to me, but Sol certainly wasn't. Sol was considered a screamer, not in the gay camp sense, but Sol screamed at his secretaries, his line producers, the technical crew, agents, lawyers. In fact, Sol screamed to the point of keeping a throat spray in his glove compartment. He never screamed at me.

Sol considers me a piece of porcelain, the Limoges his ex-wife Irene bought and was later destroyed in the quake, the Italian dinnerware he admired at Bob Evans' Bel Air estate in the Seventies, when Ali McGraw sat silently at the table, with glazed eyes and wearing a lot of suede fringe, staring into candlelight and red wine, while Sol and Bob and Jack and Barry, and other men for whom first names are enough, discussed the profits from *Chinatown*. The sun fired itself into the Pacific, casting shadows slithering like jungle vipers into the room, and the scent of Rigand candles ate the air.

Sol has mentioned to me on many occasions how he still admires that Italian dinnerware.

'Food looks good on it. You serve dog shit on it and it looks like steak.'

'I draw the line at shit on a plate, Sol. Let's change the subject,' I countered quietly.

'What? Stop whispering!' This is Sol's standard reply.

'I said, that's enough. The conversation is in poor taste.'

'Welcome to Hollywood.' He begins to laugh. I am being tested. All the time.

We are at the intersection of Mulholland Drive and Beverly Glen, waiting on a red light, one Sol can't run. He turns and stares at me, a curious wrinkle on his cheek.

'What are you thinking about?' Sol asks me gruffly. 'You got a grin on your face.'

I leave my sunglasses on, stare ahead at traffic.

'I was thinking of two things. I was thinking about shit on a plate. Bob Evans, Italian dinnerware. *That* story. And I was thinking about what you must have been like when you were twenty-five.'

Sol puts his hand on my knee, something he's never done, then withdraws it.

'Kiddo, when I was twenty-five, I'd come four times a day. Women used to say they'd get pregnant if they sat on the same toilet seat as me.'

Sol guns the Jag as the light slowly turns green.

FOUR

SUE ELLEN TROY LOOKED like her sister. But she was taller, much thinner, her hair a deep chestnut. Sue Ellen had 'a figure'.

Sue Ellen Troy had a husband in real estate in Phoenix, Arizona, an adobe house with a pool on Camelback Mountain.

'Mr Seagull says you may want to talk to me about Kathi,' Sue Ellen said in a weary voice over the phone.

'I'll be over at the Cloud Nine most of this week,' I quietly answered.

'Are you a policeman?' Sue Ellen asked.   35

'No. A screenwriter. I'm writing for Mr Seagull. On your sister.'

'That's right. I remember now. Well, I can't tell you much about Kathi, not since she went to college. She was always a loner. Not much personality. But she tried.'

Sue Ellen, I rationalized, didn't know about shady three-bedrooms at the Cloud Nine, or the solitary life. Of watching sunsets on the Ventura Freeway in a traffic jam, breathing in the kind of vague incense that only freeways produce. Of singing along to Stevie Nicks on the FM radio and knowing all the words to 'Thunder Only Happens When It's Raining' . . . Of pushing a cart with bad wheels through Ralph's Supermarket full of ice cream, grapes, deli cheeses and pink champagne and watching the checkout girl, with burnt-blonde hair and blue contacts, cheerfully remark, 'Having a party?'

No, Kathi Kind must have thought on those summer days before her death, no, I'm not having a party.

Sue Ellen Troy's worst characteristic was not a physical one. Sue Ellen had about as much personality as wet concrete. Like her sister, Sue Ellen was made for the smaller cities, the suburbs without form. Before her husband hit it big in Phoenix, they moved from Peoria to Boise to Salt Lake City. Here intelligence and sophistication were not deciding factors in a woman's popularity; rather, where she lived, where she shopped, if she said please and thank you and cocked her head at a particularly cute angle, who her husband was and where he was going, these were the most important fences guarding the minefields small city women made for themselves.

Kathi Kind and Sue Ellen Troy were raised for this kind of life.

Sue Ellen had flown in on Tuesday and stayed in Kathi's apartment, keeping the drapes drawn and the air conditioner on full blast. Sue Ellen arranged for Kathi's services, pocketed the cash in Kathi's sewing box (almost six thousand dollars in small bills, not discovered in the heat of the murder). How did Sue Ellen know? Because her mother, and her grandmother, put their money in a sewing box, the same sewing box, of carved mahogany and a Victorian needlepoint top of a dog and a flower, stabbed with straight pins. And now this box would serve as Sue Ellen's private bank in one of the six bedrooms in her house on Camelback Mountain. It stood to reason for Sue Ellen. It made sense. She always had her eye on that box.

Sue Ellen quietly sold Kathi's furniture to the Rotellas; Mr Rotella extremely satisfied with the price, Mrs Rotella thrilled enough to fix Sue Ellen the strongest frozen daiquiri she'd ever tasted.

I had flown out the day after Kathi's demise. The money was so terrific I knew, after speaking to Seagull, that this wouldn't come up again. During that week of constant cocktails at the Cloud Nine, I taped them all. The Rotellas, June Spring, Louise Shearer, and Martin Fogelson, even Herb and Matt, who asked me if I would like to watch a little adult video with them, clothes off. Herb grinned, stating he and Matt beat off every day at four, tea time you know, and they'd love some company. I declined.

It was on the following Saturday, before Kathi's internment, that I had one last drink with the Rotellas by the pool. It was six p.m. Sue Ellen had moved to a motel on Sepulveda Boulevard as the Rotellas took the furniture as soon as they paid for it, and she was in Kathi's apartment packing up two last boxes.

38

I did not actively seek Sue Ellen out this past week. Kathi's sister was only an afterthought at this point, and I realized this is one reason why Kathi Kind lived here, on Burbank Boulevard, in the white smoke and scorched palms. She didn't want to be an afterthought. But she didn't know how not to be.

I knocked on the apartment door.

'It's open,' a flat voice whispered.

The living room was very cold, almost frigid. Only the kitchen was lit, casting a strange pearlescence through the rest of the apartment. Sue Ellen, in a pair of beige slacks and a Jaclyn Smith sweater from K-Mart, sipped a glass of tap water from the kitchen sink. The air conditioner's plastic streamers kept flapping.

'The water here's funny tasting.' Sue Ellen had her back to me.

'It's good for washing dishes, that's about it,' I murmured.

'You coming tomorrow?' Sue Ellen turned to me. I almost hoped for tears. Some kind of drama. Her face was smooth, uninterested.

'Yes.'

'You know, Kathi wanted to be put to rest at Holly-wood Memorial. I don't get it. We're not Jews, you know. I went there yesterday. The place is a dump. I saw garbage in a pond and beer bottles on Tyrone Power's grave. Lotsa Jew graves. She never liked movies all that much.'

Sue Ellen turned back to the sink and filled up another glass.

I couldn't tell her that not everything in life occurs from a repeated set of circumstances, or that every moment is made from a plan. Perhaps Kathi wanted to be remem-bered in a place where some of the most beautiful people that have ever lived are buried. Perhaps in death, by geography, she would suddenly, finally become special.

'Well, she's a bunch of ash now.'

I bit my lip and said nothing.

'You know, I always told Kathi if you want a desk job with the Feds, go to Phoenix, or Flagstaff, where your money really *goes* someplace. I know a couple in Prescott who work accounts for the Pentagon and they have the most gorgeous log house. Four bedrooms, four fireplaces! They got it for a song, live like royalty. Oh, that Susan is such a doll.'

With batteries, I thought to myself. Sue Ellen sighed, swished some water in her mouth, and spit it out in the sink.

'May I ask you a question?' I murmured.

'Sure. Shoot.'

There was a distinct silence as I thought about phrasing, tone.

'How much did Sol Seagull pay you for the rights to Kathi's life?'

Sue Ellen looked straight at me.

'A lot.'

'How much?'

'A hundred thousand.'

'What? Dollars? Yen? Pesos?' I heard my voice become sarcastic.

'Dollars, silly.' Sue Ellen's voice became perky, very sweet. She continued.

'How much he pay you to write the movie?'

'Considerably more. You should have asked for a quarter million. At least.' My voice had become very confiding and low. Sue Ellen wrinkled her mouth. I assumed this was an expression of deep thought.

41

'Well, Mr Johnson, I don't know this world of yours too good, but a hundred grand goes a long way in Phoenix, Arizona. My husband Freddie wants to build a nice shopping plaza in Tempe, across from the university, so I said, sure honey, in fact last night on the phone over at the motel I said sure. I'll own it though.'

'Of course,' I said.

'Kathi wouldn't want it any other way,' Sue Ellen decided.

No, I thought. Kathi would prefer to be alive. Slim and pretty. Living with a doctor in Beverly Hills.

'I thought you might have wanted to talk to me about Kathi and me when we were kids,' Sue Ellen said with a slight chill in her voice.

'Not really,' I countered, shifting my weight from one foot to the other. 'See, it's going to be a murder mystery. But then it'll wind up an erotic thriller.'

Sue Ellen wrinkled her lips again.

'Mr Seagull didn't say nothing about sex. I don't want Kathi looking like a tramp.'

I thought to myself, but you certainly didn't waste time coming to an agreement with Seagull, Sue Ellen Troy.

'What day did Mr Seagull make his offer? Do you remember?' I asked. I wasn't quite sure why I decided to pry. Except that when Seagull had called me it was Sunday, the evening of the discovery of Kathi Kind. Now I've heard of certain Hollywood people who kept close ties to the city coroner's office and found out the juice before the *Los Angeles Times*; the hatchet murders and starlet overdoses and stalker shootings. Strike fast. Call the bereaved before they can think twice, make a low offer and you got the rights.

'He called me that night. Sunday. Right after *Sixty Minutes*, I think. I mean, *Sixty Minutes*, Phoenix time.'

It made sense. Sol obviously wanted to show someone in Century City that he was still fast on his feet. Who was it? Sherry Lansing at Paramount? Which law firm? Which agency? I knew Sol was old-fashioned, it was studio money or no money at all. No foreign funds for Sol. Or drug money washed in the Bahamas. No one on the ladder in Hollywood cares where the money comes from, except Sol and the big boys.

Sol has always said when you reach the top you never assume. Sol also concurred that you can just watch vice presidents and studios disappear. Someone offers them a cool million to produce and they don't care if the money came from selling retarded babies to meat plants. But the guys who last, they ask where the money comes from.

And Sol always knew what would sell. He started out in real estate in the Valley about 1955; 'A good story is like a well-built house,' Sol often remarked to me with a slightly crisp tone, meant to sound intelligent, and a raised eyebrow. 'And if it's a good house,' Sol would add, 'you can sell it over and over again, each time for more.'

I turned my attention to Sue Ellen. 'Kathi seems to me to be a nice, quiet woman.'

'Been a nice, quiet woman, honey. Been,' Sue Ellen remarked coarsely. There was a silence, a hesitation born of ignorance and the snap and fizz of the air conditioning unit. Sue Ellen continued.

'She was okay. Not much to write home about,' Sue Ellen said, twisting her costume jewelry ring.

You bitch, I thought. You rot.

Sue Ellen sighed, looking around the best apartment at the Cloud Nine.

'I got to wait two weeks for the money. Mr Seagull

explained the studio signs and writes the checks, and I signed the contract on Monday. So it'll still be a couple of weeks. Are studio checks good someplace else besides Hollywood?' Sudden innocence.

'Yes,' I answered. I didn't want to explain to her what Hollywood money really is: blood money, guilt money, hush money, money she'll spend too fast, money that'll kill her marriage and middle age. How one day she'll wake up in her house up on Camelback Mountain and wonder what the hell happened.

But Sue Ellen had already decided, I soon realized, what to do with that money before her sister's head could be sewn back on.

'I like the weather in Phoenix,' Sue Ellen said in a monotone. 'It's drier. Not so dirty and damp.'

Then go back as soon as possible, I said to myself. No one will miss you either.

I didn't say goodbye, but walked back out to the pool. A high, hot wind was stirring the bamboo.

'Well! Back for a fresher-upper?' Mrs Rotella poured me a ginger ale and walked over to me with a big smile on her face.

45

'Whatdya think of Sue Ellen? Nice gal, huh?' Mr Rotella asked.

'The furniture looks just lovely, honey.' Mrs Rotella patted her husband's wrinkled brown face. I could hear June Spring put a record on upstairs, Alice Faye singing 'Blue Moon'. The wind became almost fierce, shaking the table and striped red and yellow umbrella where the Rotellas made drinks. I listened to the crackle of bamboo, growing louder in the dusk as I sipped my ginger ale. I thought I could hear a woman's voice, a laugh, a whisper.

'Get a load of that sunset,' Mrs Rotella said dreamily. The sky was on fire, orange and peach.

'Yeah. Get a load of it,' I said to the Rotellas, smiling. I'll remember this sunset, I thought, long after there's a reason to.

FIVE

'A TELEPHONE CALL AT three o'clock in the *mañana*. See how much I love you?'

'I know you do, Sol,' I whisper.

There is a long silence. Palm trees rustle in an early morning breeze. Two of my palms are in bloom, and the flowers, like wasps, drift through the night air towards the still-lit pool.

'Just this. I still like the hip Jack the Ripper thing. Call it *Stranger At The Door*, and don't set it at such a shitty apartment. It should be a house in the hills, get it? City glittering below, sunsets.'

'Kathi couldn't afford a house in the hills, Sol.'

'We change that. She's a successful business consultant with a house in the hills. She's alone because she's getting over the end of a passionate relationship.'

'Jesus.'

'He doesn't work in Hollywood, sweetheart. Also make her a blonde, and I think we could get Kelly Lynch.'

'Kathi Kind was overweight and alone.' I realize my voice does not sound pleased.

'Well, she ain't now, kid. Write a shower scene in, at least for a couple seconds of tits. She's hot, she's tired from male chauvinist executives, so once the door is closed, she strips and gives herself a good soaping and then she hears something . . .'

'This isn't what happened, Sol.'

'Who gives a shit what happened? I own her now. I own her life. And I own her death, too. Fair and square.'

I pause, shiver.

'Well, Sol, I must admit, it's not too terribly original. You have a good budget and this sounds like direct to video.'

'Fuck. Well, you're the writer.' Sol hangs up.

I look through my notes from the late summer, trying to find a sense of how the murder took place. The visual dynamics of the scene are going to need tremendous silence and suspense. Maybe a little music, I think. A zither, a heartbeat, and the door to Kathi Kind's ultra-sleek, grey and pink Hollywood Hills house, with a city-lights view and night-lit swimming pool, begins to creak open. The hand opening it is encased in a black leather glove. No, too OJ Simpson.

The hand opening the door is wrinkled and large, a man's hand, but the nails are press-on and a distinct shade of red. There is a large diamond ring, a woman's ring, on the wedding finger. No, too *Dressed To Kill*.

A hand in a white gardener's glove opens the door. Fine. Anonymous. We hear the background become tense, strung out. The camera goes through the dark house until it reaches the bedroom. We can hear the sound of a shower. A lot of jump cuts to Kathi Kind sensually soaping her large, perfect breasts and adorable bush. Oh God, this stinks.

I look again through my notes.

The only unusual factor in the last six months of Kathi

Kind's life was that she had switched jobs, moving slightly up the ladder, from her job at Social Security to an assistant accountant at a film studio. Even then, Kathi was less interested in the movie business than in the fact she'd be earning a dollar more an hour and the studio, in Burbank, was only six blocks down from her old office. This made sense. Kathi liked the change, and the money, and she was very pleasant and perky to all the gals at the office, not the pretty ones looking to marry a film executive, but the gals like her, who expected wide chairs, air conditioning, and extra coffee breaks.

Suddenly I realize, with the most simple of shocks, a sigh mixed with a shudder, that Kathi Kind was murdered by someone at the studio. Someone who watched her finding her way around, smiling, a cup of coffee in her hand.

SIX

FUNNY HOW YOU CAN'T come up with excuses at a funeral.

The afternoon light at Hollywood Memorial is adulterous, made for sunglasses and the quiet click of motel doors. If I were still an alcoholic I would wave my hand about my face, mumble about a hangover. Mumble about the auto exhaust from Santa Monica over the stone faces of angels.

I am walking towards the Court of the Apostles, where Kathi Kind's ashes are to be interred, past Tyrone Power's monument, past Cecil B. DeMille and the dozens of much lesser directors whose widows paid big bucks to have their husbands buried near him, as location is *everything*.

Imagine having a stone movie camera, its dials and face beginning to smooth down over your grave, with your name on it, and all the biggest films you directed listed in alphabetical order. If not kept up, it'll wind up looking like a prehistoric bird.

I'm sober, too sober, to revel in this decay. All I know, this afternoon light is where you get *caught*.

Imagine screwing the wrong person, walking outside with a smile on your face, and seeing their lover coming towards you with a gun, a faceless enemy in the late afternoon, barely visible through your dark black 'I'm having an affair' sunglasses, and you know in a minute you're going to die.

The light is orange and titty pink, uncontrolled and heavy. There is a boombox blaring Boyz II Men down the street, and you think, I'm destined to repeat this. In my next life I will be shot in the late afternoon, my funeral will be held in the late afternoon and the same contingent of the damned will show up, wearing the same

black clothes they nightclubbed in less than twelve hours

before. I'm destined to die from a love song in the late afternoon, a faint psalm in the air. I'm destined to cause jealousy and be its victim. I'm destined to be discovered, to be caught, and that is the final, unreturnable sin of Los Angeles. Here you live your life one step ahead. You aren't supposed to backtrack. Only losers get caught.

I take in a deep breath and return my attention to the funeral. We are at the Court of the Apostles, it's marble, cool and almost damp, a pleasant surprise. There are more people here than I expected. Sol Seagull is wearing a finely tailored navy blue Italian suit.

There is always a whiff of the Fifties and Sixties around Sol, a golf-shoed, country club feel that spells out safety, long life, good liquor, fine women and sunny skies.

He's probably the most evil person I know, but I love him. In fact, I've thought I would sleep with him if he asked me to. I'm his token queer, and we get alone fine, and sometimes he puts his gesturing hand, the one with the ruby from Bulgaria, on my knee. I know he's playing with me. And I know he's looking just beyond me, the next target, bullseye, thin paper sheet with a man's outline.

I allow myself this strange fetish, and I allow Sol his ruthlessness. This is how business is done in Hollywood. Never bring business home, but you can bring it into bed, as long as that bed is someplace where you won't get caught.

Sol has the kind of rosy satisfaction a serial killer must experience when he remembers to clean the meat cleaver and put it back into the drawer.

'Thanks for everything, Mr Seagull.' Sue Ellen Troy is wearing a black polyester pants suit and a black straw hat. She shakes Sol's hand, takes a deep breath.

'They made the hands and neck look like, well, you know, like nothing happened.'

'Mr Frannino is a genius. All the top people use him.'

Sue Ellen turns to me and says, in a flat voice, 'Hi again.'

I feel suddenly like a co-conspirator and I try to decide for what. I manage a wan smile.

Sue Ellen continues. 'It was very strange to see her casket roll down that little moving thing into the flames.

Mother and Father were buried, just like everybody else.'

'Well, Kathi wanted Hollywood Memorial, and the only space available is number 463 in the north wing of the Court. And that's only for ashes, dear.' Sol has a way of making this sound like ordering a Mustang in violet. Somehow soothing.

Sue Ellen looks around.

'Kathi never had a lot of friends, you know. It's nice to see so many attractive, glamorous people.'

Sol nods his head sweetly as Sue Ellen walks to the front of the folding chairs. It has gotten hot. People are fanning themselves.

'Central Casting,' Sol whispers to me. 'These will be extras in the funeral scene when the film rolls. They're getting paid, and we keep them on file until the shoot.'

'Jesus.'

'So what's the big deal?' Sol grunts.

'This is just like the beginning of *The Bad And The Beautiful*,' I whisper.

'The *what*?'

'A movie from 1952. With Kirk Douglas and Lana Turner.'

55

'What makes you think I'm interested in some old black-and-white with Lana Turner?'

'How did you know it was black-and-white?' I sound surprised.

'Odds. You know about odds, Samuel.'

'Here and there.'

'Just the odds, kiddo.'

'In *The Bad And The Beautiful*, the first time we see Kirk Douglas, he is paying off a group of extras that have made up the audience at his film producer father's funeral. Apparently his father was not well-liked.'

'Jeez, here all this time I thought I was the first one to do it. Goddamit.'

I cannot seriously explain to Sol that everything that happens in Hollywood in real life has happened before in a film, mostly forgotten films. I cannot explain to him that evil is incapable of original thought, but only repeats itself. And I cannot explain anything I see anymore.

'You look very handsome today, Sam. A real gentleman,' Sol says in a soft voice.

'Thanks, Sol.'

'It's nothing.'

This is unusual. I reason. I sincerely doubt Sol is impressed by my literary scope, as talent here refers to day players and not what a person is born with.

Sol takes off his Giorgio Armani sunglasses and I gulp some air. His eyes are a stunned, flickering green, tired and pink-rimmed. I like Sol's eyes. This is the first time I've ever seen them.

'What do you say we get drunk after this? Funerals. I don't like funerals.'

'I don't drink.'

'Will you smoke some dope with me?'

I give this some thought.

'Maybe.'

'Tell you what. I have an answer print on *Femenina*. We can have Corbin screen it at Universal. We'll have the entire screening room. The door locks. We can toke up and have some laughs. The film stinks so bad we'll have to spray the place with Lysol.'

'Maybe, Sol. I'll watch the movie with you. See, I have to keep a firm sense of being in control of myself. I can't always . . .'

'Oh, please. Loosen up.' It is a command.

57

A minister gets up and we all rise, then sit down.

'Don't tell me, Sol, the minister is not church ordained.'

'Central Casting.'

'Jesus.'

'He's trying out for me. Listen, he's a great character man. Works all the time. Sends me a birthday card every year.'

It is August twenty-third. Just beyond our staged memoriam, with a fine character man speaking of Kathi's warm heart and civic responsibility (and Sue Ellen ready to hop on a plane to Phoenix from the front row) I hear a rustling of silk. A group of women in heavy black veils are moving towards the plaque of Rudolph Valentino in the marble wall. Some hold a single lily, a white rose. Some are crying, holding a Bible and black beads. There are photographers from the *Star*, the *Enquirer*, and *Midnight*, busy taking flash pictures.

'The Lady in Black,' Sol says in an amused, low voice.

'Yes, Sol. The mysterious Lady in Black. Who came to Valentino's crypt, every year, on the anniversary of his death.'

'Well, that's today, Samuel.'

'Oh my God.'

'It's great publicity.'

I look closer. There must be close to forty women in black. A tape is playing as the tears begin to flow; 'There's a New Star in Heaven Tonight – R-u-d-y – V-a-l-e-n-t-i-n-o,' sung by Rudy Vallee. The song is beginning to echo.

The mourners at Kathi Kind's interment turn their film-extra faces and stare at the Valentino soirée, whispering and giggling. Sue Ellen only looks confused.

I realize all those women, or the majority of them, are men in drag; their heels are very high, tapping the marble like castanets. The clothes are too sexy, the makeup under those heavy veils thicker than most showgirls'.

Somehow, I know this is right. That in the long, eternal run, it would be nice to have a series of drag queens mourning my memory to music, in the middle of summer, in a mausoleum. With photographers. I smile, turn and look at Sol. He is scowling at the minister, who is beginning to drone.

'Fucking enough already.'

I think of Ramon Navarro, who kept a lack-lead, Art Deco dildo embellished with Rudolph Valentino's silver signature, next to his bed. This was the same dildo used to kill Navarro, by two hustlers named Paul Robert Ferguson and Thomas Scott Ferguson. Ramon Navarro, one of the most beautiful young men in the world, the original 'Ben Hur', grew old and forgotten in Hollywood, and wound up with that dildo shoved down his throat, dead.

The hustlers' explanations:

'He was old, man.'

'See, a hustler is someone who can talk – not just to men, to women, too. Who can cook. Can keep company. Wash a car. Lots of things make up a hustler. There are a lot of lonely people in this town, man.'

'He was an old queer, man.'

'He deserved to die.'

Sol interrupts my thoughts. He is becoming bored, agitated. The air in the Court of the Apostles is heavy with Chantilly and Arpege, clouds of it, but not from our memoriam. Sol clears his throat and speaks.

'You know, this isn't a town for white people. Never really was. Well, maybe during all that building between the two wars.'

Sol and I watch the drag queens, in line, walk out of the mausoleum in a sort of state funeral elegance. Many hold small handkerchiefs under their veils, dabbing their eyes.

'I beg your pardon?' I ask.

'That's a white person's remark. You're too damn white, Samuel. You need to be more of a hustler. Hustlers don't say, "I beg your pardon?" They say, "What's it to you?" Or, "Let's get down to dollars." Not, "I beg your pardon."'

'I'm not following you,' I say quietly. Sol adjusts his hearing aid.

'What?'

'I'm not following you.'

'Oh. Just you got to understand. Jews control Hollywood. It's ours, not yours. What we didn't get in Israel we got here, baby, and it's OURS. Los Angeles was built by niggers and Jews and Mexicans and everywhere they took and took. Each one of them a hustler, Samuel.'

I still don't understand Sol's sudden shift in focus. The minister stops, sympathetically shakes the outstretched

61

hand of a numbed Sue Ellen, and heads down the aisle towards Sol, who keeps his eye on Sue Ellen.

'How'd I do, chief?' the minister says in a stage whisper.

'Fine, Brett. Call my secretary in the morning. She'll set you up.'

An attendant, a wiry, small woman with cheekbones like a vulgar small bird, puts Kathi's ashes in their final resting place.

Sue Ellen checks her lipstick with a pocket mirror which she drops back into her purse. She speaks quietly to the attendant, and Kathi's mourners do not wish Sue Ellen well, but walk past Sol and me, apprehension and excitement in their faces.

'Yes, you were great,' Sol mutters, with a certain contemptuous patience, as they each walk by.

'Shit, is there a back door here?' Sol asks in an exhausted voice, turning to me.

'I'm sure there must be,' I say.

I discovered the dichotomy of my life when I realized there was a back door to everything. At the amusement parks of my youth I loved rollercoasters. I loved their white paint and swaying wood as the cars plummeted down and I loved the screams, the slap of air and gravity, the way the bravest held their arms up under the summer sun, not holding on to the safety bars.

What I found out later is that even rollercoasters have a back entrance for staff, an alley covered in weeds. The paint isn't quite as white on that side, and the wood seems old, ready to fall apart. In those alleys and under those tracks, there are men in striped, hot shadows and flies, their pants around their knees, groaning with each other.

This I discovered when I was fourteen, and suddenly what was hidden became much more interesting to me than what I could see.

Sol is walking around the mausoleum, craning his neck. With his insolent strut and his expensive shoes. I assume this marble gallery of bones does not amuse him. For once it is something he cannot own. Then I judge the service: Sol paid for it, hired the actors, bought the flowers, bought Kathi Kind's life. Yes, he does own the place.

He almost looks like those men behind the rollercoaster, I muse. Except not as desperate. Sol's older, yes, I say to myself, but he's fairly muscular, his tan is perfect, his hair like fresh snow. I suddenly wonder again if he wears underwear, what side he dresses to, if he has tattoos. This and what he is like, or must have been like, when he comes.

This is a bad alley, Samuel, I suddenly realize, and you better get on the main drag fast. Even the idea I could be attracted to an older man, a shrewd horror with too much cash and a sadistic sense of control, terrifies me. The smell of death is all around me and it is not damp and sweet. It is dry and reeking of dust and auto exhaust and brittle flowers and unwashed marble.

I walk up to Kathi Kind's simple plaque, made out of pot metal painted to resemble bronze, and four posts, one at each corner, with brand new, shiny round-head screws.

I realize I have only moments before Sol is back. In a mausoleum, those slow moments of inactivity are much like what a child feels sitting in the back of a car, moving along a highway. Time is suspended. The road rolls out into an adult nothingness.

I notice only one Lady in Black is left sitting on a

folding chair next to Valentino's tiny crypt. Incense is burning. A tape of Maria Callas singing *Tosca* has taken over the hall. The Lady in Black's gloved hands reach out to a shaft of light, yellow with afternoon's spit, that is quietly making its way across the floor, hitting her pointed, black lace, heels.

'Rudy. Rudy. *Mi amore. El finale, el muerte.*' The voice is a deep man's voice, a mature man, say about fifty years old. Still too young, I think, to be the Lady in Black.

Callas starts hitting her high notes in *Tosca*, her voice demonic, exquisite. The shaft of light moves past the Lady in Black. She shrugs, turns the tape off, gathers up her things. There is a lovely sigh in her deep, masculine voice.

'Rudy, no one understands. No one understands.'

This *mise en scène* is played perfectly, I realize. As the Lady in Black moves past me with a regal nod, I see hair under the nylons on her legs, a moustache under her black chiffon veil, heavy eyebrows, a blackish shadow on her cheeks, and perfectly painted, ruby red lips. Like the petals of an over-ripe rose.

I now see that no matter how many people want to be you, the only way you'll ever be noticed, and believed, is to be the first, or the last, of your kind. Start it or end it, but never allow yourself to be caught in the middle. I also know I just saw the Lady in Black, not a hairy old drag queen, but the real item, because she waited it out, her script was memorized, and no matter what, she was the last one to leave.

Like those old men behind the rollercoaster. Like those old, old men in the back of porno theaters and all-night movie houses in New York and Miami, men waiting for the perfect cock, the big squirt and sigh in the flickering darkness.

I remember never being frightened of them. I remember my young penis with its little tuft of hair, hard as cement. It was never, 'Come here, little boy,' but more, 'Want to have some fun, want to feel good, let me help you.' And I did let them help me, and it felt good, and no one was ever cruel. I thought, as my teenage years idly sank from memory, that I had done them a favor. Now I see it was instinct, and besides my revulsion at their age, the hands covered with liver spots, the thick glasses, dentures, hairpieces, glass eyes, wrinkled fore-heads, there was also a sense of jealousy. I thought, they must blow a lot of guys like me. Think of the penises they must see; the fun they must have. I wouldn't know, because I always pulled up my pants and fled. But those old men, they were the last of their species, and always the last to leave.

Sol is whistling. I hear the echo. A homeless woman is sitting in another part of the Court of the Apostles, tossing bits of her sandwich to a mountain of small ants. She does not laugh. Her movements are machine-like.

Suddenly I have to be outside, and taste the warm California sun. They're going to make a movie about you, Kathi, I think to myself. They're going to change everything and I'm writing it. Half the cast was here today to see you off, Kathi, even your sister, Sue Ellen. You're going to be a movie star, not forgotten after all.

There is a siren on Santa Monica Boulevard, vague and

whirling in a high-pitched cackle. I look for Sol, and I find him at the end of a long marble hall.

'Here we go. You were right, kid. Here's a back door.'

SEVEN

I AM SITTING IN the Hitchcock Theater at Universal. It feels strange, just Sol and me, in a huge plush red private screening room.

'I hate Universal. Too many goddamn vice presidents. There's a vice president for everything. Hell, they got vice presidents for the executive washroom, people to blow you and wipe your ass at the same time.' Sol coughs up some phlegm into a handkerchief.

'I sincerely doubt that, Sol,' I say, as the lights dim.

'*Femenina*. You want to talk fast? This film is so bad that three weeks ago, when we wrapped, I said to the editor, how long till an answer print? He said, three weeks, Sol, you and I know it's a piece of shit. He was right.'

'What is it about me that you like?' I turn to Sol. He grins.

'You write the script the way I want it. You're not Hollywood, you don't belong here. I know we'll shake hands and you'll get your money, then go back to the farm in Massachusetts or wherever the hell you live. I won't have to HEAR from you.'

'Thanks.'

'But see, the difference, Samuel, is I'll call you again, for another project. You'll make even more money, you'll put up with my bullshit, deliver the goods, and fly back to reality.'

'Reality?' I whisper.

'You know what I am saying.'

I look at Sol closely. His face is certainly corrupt, full of avarice, time and lines everyone's seen before. A certain exhaustion, like the Los Angeles air, with its yellowed veneer, that makes fresh flowers immediate has-beens.

I turn and watch the film. It is not as bad as Sol thinks. The female lead, Paula North, is a radiant blonde, like Marilyn before she died, just ethereal and gorgeous. She has high cheekbones and full lips, and spun-cotton, candy-blonde hair.

Sol is sucking in air between his teeth.

'You know, that girl's not bad. She dates my son.'

We watch Paula North, dressed in a brown leather trenchcoat with nothing else on except a pair of four-inch alligator heels, take a gun and shoot her mother, played by Tuesday Weld, to death. It takes five shots. In the movie, the Gypsy Kings are playing something fast and furious, very dark. A fire is roaring in the fireplace. Before committing the act, we see Paula North take a glass of brandy and throw it in the flames, wheeling around in a pitch of high drama, screaming, 'Can't you see, Mother, I'm a woman crying out?'

I blink. There is nothing like high camp to get me going.

'Jesus,' Sol says, and rolls his eyes.

'No. Wait a minute. Sol, what's wrong with this picture is the title. You've got your ads right there. Retitle it.'

'What?'

'Well, *Femenina* sounds stupid, an art-house flop.'

'And?'

'Call it *A Woman Crying Out.*'

'Uh-huh. Sounds right.' Sol's tone of voice has changed. He's thinking.

'A Woman Crying Out!' I holler in the darkness. 'Make it so bad it's good. Let everyone *know* it's trash.'

'I can do that.'

'Add some scenes, make it just utterly *appalling.*'

'I can do that.'

'You'll get the gay crowd, the students, the retirees. People love camp. They want to *laugh.*'

'You're smart. I like it,' Sol says.

'So this is still a rough cut. This isn't the answer print,' I say to myself quietly.

'What do you know about answer prints?' Sol asks me cryptically.

On the screen Paula North has been abducted by a group of Mexican gang members. They have her naked in the back seat of their Chevy Impala and are rubbing ice on Paula's exceedingly pink nipples. She is bargaining

72

with them, screaming for mercy. All the gang members sound just like Cheech Marin, I realize.

'I know an answer print is seen by executives before it is sent out to be copied. It is the one time a film looks its best, no scratches, where the editing, focus, color, sound are all at their sharpest. It's film at its purest.'

'Bullshit. Film at its purest is when the checks roll in. *That's* film.'

'I know an answer print is seen by only a few people in this world, sort of like a ninety carat diamond from Harry Winston. Only the privileged few, who get to say yes, the public will buy this, or no, shelve it and call the accounting department.'

'Or else they might say, add some truly appalling scenes and . . .' Sol laughs fiercely.

'I know an answer print is like the moment when a film has formed, it is all grown up, it has had its coming out party, its bar-mitzvah, whatever. It is still virginal.'

'Virginal? Honestly, Samuel.'

'No, listen. Soon there will be ten thousand copies of an answer print. They will become scratched and faded. Then video. But for a little while, this celluloid is pure as a just-squeezed tube of oil paint. Like a teenage girl who, quite simply, will never be as beautiful again. The picture always fades.'

'Oh God, poet rising.'

'It's when the celluloid is still mystery. Unborn. Perfect. When a movie star, in all that crispness, that perfect sound and color, is really a movie star.'

Sol puts his hand to his chin and rubs it.

'So what you're saying, Samuel, is we aren't watching this broad get her tits pinched on an answer print. We aren't watching rushes, either. Just a rough cut. It still needs more.'

'Exactly.' I let out a long breath and sink into my seat. I suddenly realize that since I was a child, waiting for the darkening of the theater, that smoky blue scene when the sparkling curtains pull slowly back, and the light beams on, that I was expecting an answer print, perfection, beauty. Every time. Foolish boy.

Sol watches *Femenina* with a kind of detachment; then says, in a monotone, 'Well, you learn something new every day. Fuck.'

74   I chuckle, raise my eyes to the screen. Paula North

now has a gag in her mouth. She is in a warehouse. There are a lot of guns being shot in the distance. Paula struggles. Her breasts shake.

'Well, kid, you told me news. Now I'll tell you one.'

'What, Sol?'

'I like the way you think. I suppose you're some kind of poet, even though I don't know cunt about poetry. Do you know what a golden moment is?'

'No.'

We are both staring at the screen, listening to each other's voices.

'A golden moment, when you're really lucky in Hollywood, is when everything goes your way. Look at Tom Cruise. Or Brad Pitt. Stallone has *had* his golden moment. He's old, a joke. But he still thinks it's happening.'

'As in how?'

'It's the moment you win your Oscar. It's the moment you sign that five-picture deal, when you have a *staff*, when you buy the biggest house in Bel Air. When everything you do is applauded. Talked about. You have to hold on to it, because it doesn't last for ever, maybe five years tops. And while you're up there, everyone you've ever known, every shitty affair, every bad deal, will be there with their hands open, waiting for you. And once they can break through the gold, baby, once they have their hands in your pockets, it's all downhill. I know guys who'll kill their wives and kids to get to that spot, that moment of gold. Guys with knives clenched between their teeth. Guys with disease and three-piece suits and brand-new Bentleys. It's the reason we're here. Fuck art, Samuel. Fuck cinema. It's the reason we're here. For the gold, baby, for the gold.'

'I can't agree with you, Sol.'

'So why do you write screenplays for me, Samuel? For the money, right?'

'I suppose so.'

'You don't *suppose* anything. For the money, right?'

'Right.'

'For the money. The extras at the funeral got paid. Sue Ellen's hitting Phoenix with a hundred grand. For the money.

'You want to win an Oscar someday, Samuel, don't you?' He hisses my name. I am not amused by our addressing each other during this conversation. Samuel,

Sol. Sol, Samuel. It's the way enemies speak, or people who are parting ways.

'Not on one of your projects, Sol. That's *not* going to happen.'

Sol laughs. Reaches for a theater phone.

'Kill the film, Hank. Raise the houselights. How's the wife? That's good.' Sol whispers conspiratorially, 'I've known Hank for twenty-five years. Otherwise, you know, we wouldn't get the Hitchcock Theater. It's just for A product.'

Poor Sol. Nothing he has ever approached me with has been A product. From what I can see, everything Sol produces seems to be borderline. Borderline B, borderline A. Moneymakers.

Sol turns to me and blinks, then puts on his sunglasses. He takes his hand and touches my cheek. A gesture that surprises. A gesture I've been hoping for, somehow.

'There are things you want, Samuel. Money first. Don't be a fool, Samuel. You don't come to Hollywood for your aesthetics. See the picture clearly. Take some Windex and clean off the glass. You're in it for the money.'

I have nothing to say. Sol puts his arm around my shoulder.

'You'll see a few answer prints, Samuel. If you decide to stick around long enough.'

The Hitchcock Theater is as quiet as the Court of Apostles. I think to myself, Samuel, you've had quite a day. Sol's voice interrupts, coming through like a rifle.

'Why don't you come over to my house for dinner tonight, Samuel? Just us, my wife, my son Joshua. And that Paula North.'

'Okay,' I shrug. I have to remember I am only visiting. Someday, as Sol pointed out, I shall go back East to wherever the hell I live.

Sol is an old man in his sixties, I remind myself. He's straight, with a wife, grown children, a membership at the Hillcrest Country Club. I am in my forties, but I still think of myself as twenty-five. This is my gay failing; assuming that I am still young and desirable, which I am not.

This is probably why I cannot find companionship.

After thirty, gay and bisexual men become invisible. They are no longer wanted. Or sought out.

Is this why I am attracted to this horror? Perhaps it is, to an Ivy Leaguer like me, a *raison d'être*. I was always told you aren't really Hollywood until you've fucked a producer.

So I fuck an old, washed-up producer who's still hanging on. He's easier to get to than the twenty-seven-year-old hotshots in Giorgio Armani, with little round wire sunglasses and a distinct lack of intelligence, or personality. In Hollywood, personality and intelligence are something you bring out when the moment is right. It reminds me of a remark by Lillian Hellman, who stated, after a dinner with Irving Thalberg and Norma Shearer, that Ms Shearer had a face 'unclouded by thought'.

EIGHT

DINNER AT SOL'S.

The Seagull house is a large, six-bedroom Tudor in Encino with a swimming pool and jacuzzi, a paddle tennis court, a small putting green for Sol – who actually stopped playing golf years ago but keeps it for friends-investors.

Sol's Jag, his son Joshua's Jeep, and his wife Wanda's Rolls-Royce are all glittering on the circular drive, not a trace of dust, or mud, on them. There are two enormous painted bronze lions, cast most likely in Tijuana out of scrap metal, facing out from the Tudor's sixteen-foot double doors.

'We had everything made in Mexico,' Sol notes proudly, 'even the cornerstones were poured down in TJ and trucked up. Saved me a million dollars at least.'

Inside, there is a two-story entrance with marble floors, a curved staircase and a massive crystal chandelier. I am impressed with the huge, exquisite floral arrangement on the round front hall table until I realize the flowers are silk and paper. The air conditioning is freezing. I sneeze. Sol slaps me on the back.

As I look up to the top of the staircase, a fifty-year-old woman with high blonde hair, so teased it looks like it could break off, and large mabé pearl earrings, begins to make her descent.

I can tell this is a descent she enjoys making on a daily basis, walking regally down that curved staircase, just like Joan Crawford, Vivien Leigh, Lana Turner, and every other actress who's ever discovered an interesting doorway or a set of stairs.

However, this woman's walk is not elegant, but opulent. She has large breasts encased in a lacy French bra that can be easily seen through her Gucci see-through blouse, and her Gucci black velvet bell-bottoms are a tad too tight for a fifty-year-old. With each step the breasts quiver, the fanny moves from side to side.

Sol sighs. It is apparent to me he married this woman and built this staircase for precisely this daily vision.

Wanda is her name, and Wanda wears creamy makeup that glistens in the light of the big chandelier. Lips somewhere between red and pink, false eyelashes, immaculate eye shadow. She has languid eyes, the kind of eyes that are never surprised.

'Nice to meet you, Sam,' Wanda says in a husky, I've-been-in-Hollywood-a-lot-longer-than-you kind of voice. 'Drink before dinner?'

'Perrier?' I ask quietly.

'Sam's a drunk,' Sol says.

'How about club soda?' Wanda murmurs, leading us into the bar area.

'Fine.'

Wanda turns and looks at me.

'Oh, by the way, bright eyes, before Sol says it, I've had everything done. Twice. So at dinner you won't have to bother finding the marks behind my ears. I don't like being stared at. At least not for that.'

'Click,' I say.

Wanda looks at me, puzzled.

Sol interjects. 'It's a nigger term. Means he understands.' Sol slaps my back again. I do not like it. I promise myself the next time he tries this I shall duck.

'I didn't know it was a black expression,' I say as Wanda hands me my drink, 'I just heard a kid use it in a movie and I thought it was cute.'

'Uh-huh,' says Wanda, smiling ruefully. Wanda bends over to find a bottle of Glenlivet Scotch, and Sol throws a peppermint at her rear end.

'Very funny, Sol.'

It is the first time I've ever heard Sol giggle. A true giggle, like a schoolboy. Wanda opens the bottle of Glenlivet with the kind of lush grace I used to have, and pours two tall drinks, one for her and one for Sol. Soda water. A squeeze of lemon. Then the ice, dropped in one cube at a time, until the drinks are frosty. This girl is an expert.

'We're having lobster, Sam. You like lobster?'

'I love lobster,' I say brightly.

'See, Sol never ever takes the family out for a meal at

a restaurant. Oh no, he says, too expensive, bad service. So instead I learnt how to buy wholesale. Lox and caviar, lobster, roast beefs. We have gourmet every night. I try to figure out ways to make the dining room *look* different. Anything, you know?' Wanda sighs.

'Can it, Wanda,' Sol hisses.

Wanda smirks. 'But the big problem is staff. None of these Spics speaks English. I get a live-in couple, they last a week. These people were shitting in holes down in Nicaragua. They don't know what a toilet is. Or how to clean it. Or what a garbage disposal is. I have to *teach* them everything.'

'Tell the English nanny story,' Sol cuts in, shaking the ice in his drink.

Wanda shivers, sips her Scotch. 'Well, I had no help for a week. Sol had to show me how to make a sandwich and I cut my finger. Had to be taken to the hospital. Ten stitches. I was very depressed.'

'Oh dear,' I say, crossing my legs.

'I get a call from this employment agency I use. Says there's an older woman, an English nanny, needs a job. Very gentle with kids. They don't mention animals, and

I think Wanda, the kids are grown, but you got four Chihuahuas, and not everyone *likes* Chihuahuas.'

'Where are they?' I ask. 'I like Chihuahuas.'

'Upstairs in the bedroom,' Sol states gruffly. 'Behind locked doors.'

'So she comes over for an appointment. Lovely, solid, big-bosomed English nanny type, just like the agency said. Beautiful, elegant accent. Besides cleaning, says she can cook, too. I'm thinking, good, my prayers are answered. I then ask her if little dogs bother her, and she smiles and says she *loves* little dogs. So I hire her.'

Wanda's eyes glaze over momentarily. She inhales quite a bit of Scotch, and sets her drink down on the bar.

'So I take her to the staff quarters and show her to her little apartment. I explain where the linen and towels are, and I tell her I'll be in later once she's settled in. For the next few hours I hear odd little noises around the house, but I don't think anything of it. Around cocktail hour I knock on her door. Sam, when she opened that door I just about died.'

Pause. I uncross my legs.

'She'd hung up black draperies. There were black

candles and she had moved the rug away and painted a black pentagram on the floor. My little Chihuahua, Twinkles, was moaning and tied to the floor in the middle of the pentagram. There was this weird tape of Satanic chants and moaning. Well, she had a knife, a big knife from *my* kitchen, in her hand. I just started screaming. I told her she was fired, I didn't want a Satanist maid, and to give me back Twinkles this instant. I really raised my voice, you know. I told her I'd called a taxi and I wanted her out of my house, not tomorrow, not tonight, but now. I untied Twinkles and grabbed the roast beef knife from her and fled.'

'She was hysterical.' Sol smiles. 'Wanda called me at the studio, told me the story, I came right home. Turned out this witch needed to use the phone, so Wanda and I listened in on the line. This witch calls one of her girl-friends, says she doesn't understand America, that she always thought it was free from religious persecution, but she's not allowed to even practise her own religion, and that this horrible woman with breast implants and two-inch nails became violent with her, and now she fears for her life, and she's leaving pronto.'

'Don't you just *love* it?' Wanda asks, sighing. 'But Twinkles is still alive and well, thank God.'

'Let me take you into the kitchen,' Wanda says with pride.

I decide it would be impolite to say no, and as I have been judging what exactly passes for good manners in Sol Seagull's house, I get up cheerfully, and say, 'You know, these Los Angeles mansions are always quite a mystery to me. They're so big, so many rooms.'

'Wait till you see my kitchen.'

Wanda's kitchen is entirely done in black marble: walls, countertops, floors. There are copper and steel restaurant-size ovens and refrigerators, copper pans hanging from the ceiling, a fireplace, a breakfast area with a black marble oval table and teakwood chairs, two different cooking islands, a living area with a black suede couch and club chairs, along with a fifty-inch television and entertainment center, a chandelier of Czechoslovakian crystal, and four black marble statues of naked Greek athletes on black marble pedestals.

'Jesus,' I whisper.

'I tried to make it as cosy as possible. Kitchens are

meant to produce good food, Sam, and this one is a twenty-four-hour workhouse.'

I look to the far end of the kitchen, which is quite far away indeed, and I see a tiny Hispanic woman with braided hair standing on a Plexiglas stool (no wood here) grabbing live lobsters out of a wet cardboard box and dropping them, one by one, into a huge pot of boiling water. The lobsters scream and the little woman claps her hands, dancing on her stool.

'She likes the sound of them screaming,' Wanda says noncommittally.

At the other end of the kitchen, a little closer to us, a Japanese man with horned-rimmed glasses and a crew cut is sharpening knives. With great fanfare Wanda introduces me to him.

'Sam, this is Hiro. Hiro cuts meat like no one else on the West Coast. He's going to do a side of lamb right now. You're in for a real treat.'

What I notice is that Hiro cannot keep his eyes off Wanda's breasts, and Wanda has a way, around this Asian knife man, of folding her arms in front of her so they pop out even more.

89

Hiro gestures to Wanda and me, and the three of us open Wanda's custom deep freeze, which is the size of most people's master bedroom.

Inside it's cold and a deathlike shade of dark blue. On hooks I see half a cow, skinned lambs still with the heads, great buckets of intestines, frozen boxes of salmon, shellfish and big silver mackerel, their dead eyes staring up at me. Also three headless, plucked ducks, a full metal bookcase piled high with prepackaged whole chickens.

Hiro takes a lamb and brings it out to the kitchen and his knives.

'Now watch,' Wanda says in awe.

I don't like looking at this lamb's dead eyes and exposed teeth, but the head is the first to go anyway. With a large cleaver Hiro cuts off the head, neatly brushing it into a bag attached to the counter for just this purpose.

'Not a thing you can do with a lamb's head,' Wanda notes, 'a cow, you've got the brains, the tongue, but a lamb has just a useless head.'

'I see.'

'Hiro, I want four good leg roasts, lightly sliced so when it cooks it puffs up. And as many thin, small chops as you can do. Not too thick, because lamb, if it's served thick, smells on the plate. Save the kidneys, the liver, the heart. Oh, Hiro,' Wanda coos, touching one of his knives and letting her breasts slightly jiggle, 'if you can scrape any bone marrow, please do. My little Chihuahuas just adore bone marrow.'

Suddenly Hiro's knives are coming down so fast and with such grace it takes me by surprise. Fascinated, I watch Hiro turn this sad little carcass into four legs of lamb, around twenty chops. Wanda sighs, compliments Hiro in a honeyed voice, letting her tits almost touch his arms, which makes Hiro work even faster. And then it's done.

'Now wasn't that exciting?' Wanda says, leading me out of the kitchen.

'I've never seen that before,' I say, phlegm in my throat.

'Hiro is worth his weight in gold, you know. He always cuts at exactly the right angle. Never a bit of bone hanging around anywhere.'

'I see.'

*   *   *

Joshua floats in about fifteen minutes after Wanda's Satanist tale, with Paula North on his arm. They are wearing motorcycle jackets and T-shirts. They are both high as kites.

'Hey, Pop.'

'Hey, Josh.'

'Hiya, Mama. This is Paula.'

Paula extends her hand. Wanda does not take it, but smiles and nods her head. Paula smiles, runs her extended hand through her 'we've been driving in a convertible' hair and shivers.

'Hope you haven't caught a cold,' I say quickly, thinking, no, Paula doesn't have a cold, the Ecstasy is just kicking in. How do I know it's drugs? Experience.

They are both incredibly beautiful. Joshua is a young Jewish Hollywood prince, muscular, selfish, green-eyed, with curly black hair on his head and perfect nipples, which can be seen through his open shirt. He looks a lot like what his father must have looked like, but Joshua's eyes are doe-like and feminine. He has on a Rolex watch, a diamond ring, two rings in his right ear, sideburns, a gold tooth from a childhood accident, and no underwear.

Paula North is not wearing a bra. Her face is devoid of makeup, except a little eyeliner and the remnants of pink lipstick. Very Dusty Springfield, I think to myself. Her teeth are perfect, her eyes blue, her hips fragile. Paula North has a great body, the kind of body and vague sexuality that middle-aged movie stars and producers want to *own*, bring out for premières and charity events.

I suddenly feel very old. I know that Hollywood is composed of three different ages: the young, hip and successful, who live in bare apartments with good art, who seem to lead their lives according to the poses of a Guess Jeans ad. They either become famous or burn out, or most of all, become average. Heaven forbid. Then there are the power brokers, all over fifty, perpetually young. Hardly ever in town. And the screen teens, still under mother's well-heeled apron. These are the people who matter.

Which leaves anyone in their thirties and forties, with average looks and salaries, cast out into the wind. Like Kathi Kind, although Kathi was always background material.

For the past several weeks working with Sol on the

script, I wake up at night and hear Kathi's voice, or at least what I imagine is Kathi's voice, murmuring around my right ear. It is not a soft voice, or a sexy voice, or a particularly womanly voice. Rather, it is the voice of a next-door neighbor, or a woman in the dressing room of a big girl shop calling out for a hanger. Somewhat disappointed, but perky.

'You're doing the right thing,' Kathi echoes.

Then all I hear is the crackle of dead palm fronds. Sometimes I turn on the radio. I believe in omens; when I turn on to a song I know, it must mean something in the scope of things. The first night I heard Kathi's voice I turned on five different radio channels. They were all religious pop. I found out Christ died for my sins.

I know I am being haunted. I know I shouldn't be socializing with Sol, or Wanda, the film noir housewife, or his vapid but delicious son and girlfriend. I shouldn't be here, drinking club soda and crossing and uncrossing my legs, but here I am. I know now that Sol is the boss, that in terms of my life these people are meaningless, and that they see me in exactly the same way. No wonder people are so cool and vacant in Hollywood. Most friend-ships simply don't matter.

Wanda rises to pour herself another drink, brushing past Paula North with a feline prissiness. Joshua and Paula have sat down on the Chesterfield sofas, in a custom eggplant color, right near the bar. Paula turns to me.

'Doesn't all that smiling make your teeth ache?' I ask sweetly. Wanda spits her Scotch into the sink behind the bar and puts her hand over her mouth, stifling laughter. Sol scowls.

'She's my gold mine. My Paula,' Sol says.

Paula looks at Joshua and they both begin to laugh. Joshua lights a cigarette, wipes a tear from his eye. Paula's eyes glisten and she shakes all that blonde hair, something I assume she does much more than once a day.

'Sam had a good idea for *Femenina*,' Sol says carefully. 'Kind of *Showgirls*.'

Paula's head snaps.

'What, Sol?'

'Call it *A Woman Crying Out*. Make it a high camp flick. Like *Rocky Horror*.'

Paula scowls.

'I already thought it was.'

There is an uncomfortable silence. I listen to the bubbles in my club soda. Wanda's voice breaks through like cough syrup.

'So tell me, Sam, how are you and Sol doing on that psycho-thriller? You know, about that poor little secretary.'

'I didn't know she was a secretary,' I say archly, 'all I know is she was in accounting.'

'She worked as my secretary,' Joshua remarks, 'for about three weeks I guess. And she worked in accounting, too.'

The air in the room, even with its eighteen-foot ceiling, becomes stale.

'I didn't know that.'

'Joshua is an assistant producer on *Dead On*. You'll see it tomorrow, Sam. At the Sherman Oaks General Cinema.' Sol stretches his legs, puts his feet up on the coffee table.

'Take those shoes off, now,' Wanda says menacingly.

'I mean it, Sol. That table's an antique. So Sam, what's

this new epic from Sol Seagull going to be called?'

'No title yet.' Sol finishes his drink. Wanda stretches luxuriously out in a chair, takes a compact and lipstick out of her Gucci velvet pants, and begins to re-do her lips in slow, luxurious strokes, all the time asking me questions.

'What about *Fat Girl Goulash?*' Wanda asks, almost religiously.

'That's not funny,' I say. I'm thinking, lobsters or no lobsters, I should leave.

'You got to have a good, good title. Right, Sol? A dynamite title.'

'Right honey.'

'How about *Who Did It?*'

'That's interesting,' I remark casually.

'By the way, Sol,' Wanda says, her breasts splaying out into a black lace explosion, 'who *did* do it?' She snaps her compact shut, runs her tongue along her teeth, then smiles at her husband.

'Not a clue. Not one fucking clue.'

'Please Sol, you know how I hate it when you swear.'

97

'That's what Sam and I feel make it such a hot property. No one knows.'

'And no one cares,' I say under my breath. 'Did you know Kathi Kind well?' I ask Joshua.

'Uh, not really. She did the financing pages for the last five pages of *Dead On*.' Joshua looks at the floor, then at his father, then at his mother. Paula watches Wanda. She is fascinated.

'Oh, oh well,' I say quietly. 'I thought it might be interesting if you heard her talk about anything, you know, of interest.'

'Zero,' Joshua says, relieved.

'Why would it matter, Sam? All I did was buy the event, not the boring stuff.'

Sol and I have decided, over the past few weeks, that this would be an ideal part for an actress who's slipped a bit, say a Morgan Fairchild.

'Actually, I was thinking Paula might be great as Kathi Kind. What do you say, Paula?'

'She was fat.'

'Not anymore.'

'She had no life.'

'Not the way we've written it.'

'She was mean.'

I swallowed an ice cube. How does she know if Kathi Kind was mean?

'So what do you say, Paula? You want to stay a big movie star?'

'I'm soft core, Sol. Don't pull my chain. Soft core I am, and that's where I'll stay. You put me there.'

'Look, sweetheart, I'm offering you the lead.'

'I'll take it.' A strange, been there, done that sigh.

Joshua kisses Paula and grins his Hollywood Jewish Prince grin. Wanda rolls her eyes. I now know this is not to be a strictly sociable occasion. I keep forgetting business is in the walls, money is in the sofa, contracts are always in a bedroom drawer.

That tiny Hispanic maid comes to the doors of the bar room. She looks like she wants to say something, but instead rings a large silver bell, over and over until Wanda gets up and glares at her. The little woman scurries away, and Wanda fiddles with the back of her brassière, then turns to us in her best Loretta Young manner and says, 'The lobster is ready. Dinner is served.'

Wanda takes my arm a bit unsteadily and says, 'I like you, Sam. You're a bitch, just like me.'

'Thank you,' I murmur.

NINE

I HAVE LEFT THE screening of *Dead On*, one of Sol's films under the Corman umbrella, even though Sol won't admit to it.

'Roger's just an investor, like everyone else,' Sol grumbles.

I know this is a lie. Corman controls everything he comes into contact with. It suddenly hits me that Sol is a B-man. That he's never actually stepped into the ring and produced a film with a heavy budget and huge stars. That he doesn't know the gang at Dreamworks. And never will. But he's rich.

101

Which means I am a hack. I am an East Coast, well-paid hack in B pictures.

Dead On features Paula North, the blonde I remember from dinner and *Femenina*, as a tightrope walker in a Nineties, Cirque du Soleil-style circus who is being pursued by a crazed, highly intelligent sniper. I assume a sniper would of course be the villain. Miss North is not about to be pursued by a crazed, highly intelligent dwarf, or a crazed, highly intelligent clown.

There was only a small group at the screening, executives with calculators from a direct-to-video conglomerate who spent most of the film talking to Sol in the back row.

I notice Paula North sitting five seats away. She is dressed in black sunglasses, black leather motorcycle jackets, pink lipstick, tight black leather pants. Blonde hair. I search my brain to decide what film her psyche has sprung out of; maybe *Brigitte Bardot and Pamela Anderson Meet Godzilla*. She is scowling, her feet up on the seat in front of her.

There are oranges rolling on Mulholland Drive, having dropped from a strangely decrepit tree, and I leave the radio on in the car and stop, getting out and picking them up by the armful. There is a slick, sunny wind blowing through and I suddenly feel like a native Californian. If I knew more, I would understand we pick fruit only from the trees in our backyard, not from poised, spidery trees at the top of the hill. Or we buy our fruit prepackaged at Hughes or Ralph's. Refrigerated. Perfect.

Stevie Wonder comes on the radio, singing 'My Cherie Amour', and as I dump the remainder of the oranges I've picked into the trunk, I lean against the car and listen:

'My Cherie Amour, pretty little one that I adore, you're the only one my heart beats for, how I wish you were mine.'

I suddenly see myself as a ten-year-old boy, visiting my father and his second wife in Minnesota. I was the happiest in my life that one summer, a yellow corn, tanned-leg girl sort of summer, with lakes and fried jumbo shrimp and a hamburger stand stuck in the middle of rolling, whooshing fields and sun. Oh God, the lakes, the mosquitoes, my innocence.

I look around. The far northern hills of the San Fernando Valley are encased in a haze the wind can't move. I begin to cry. I do not belong here, and I do not know where I am.

A truck loaded with Mexicans stops near the sad old orange tree. Quickly, the truck unloads its passengers as they race towards other citrus trees in the area, armed with covered baskets. Most of the trees are on private property, but the Mexicans take the fruit so quickly they seem invisible.

The owner of the truck nods at me. I nod back. He spits on the pavement, keeping his eye on me. The song is over and the wind is hot. It's time for me to go home.

Four blocks down on Mulholland there has been a horrible accident. One car has flown off the side and has crashed somewhere below in Studio City. The woman in the other car, a pretty redhead in black bicycle pants and a lace top, has gotten out of her Porsche Turbo Carrera and is talking on a cellular phone. There is blood running down her face. All four tires from her Porsche are rolling down the hill.

She begins screaming into the phone as the Santa Anas

whip her red hair around. Suddenly she wipes her forehead and sees the blood on her hand. She drops her
cellular phone on the pavement, and sinks to her knees
in the middle of the road, crying and rocking back and
forth.

I stop my car. I run towards her.

'Did you call 911?' I ask hurriedly.

'Yes,' she says in a monotone.

'Is there anything you need?' I ask.

She looks up at me, surprised.

'Yes. I'm thirsty.'

I go back to my car, look for bottled water which I
normally have, but don't today. Then I remember the
oranges in the trunk, and bring her two juicy ones. She
takes them, one in each hand, and begins to laugh uncon-
trollably.

I understand now, that God, or what piddling knowledge I have of God, becomes quite clear, visible to the
suffered and suffering, right after a disaster. Or right after
a loss, a kind of maiming where the soul is somehow
punctured, like a tire, and air continues to escape.

That is when God comes, in the white cumulus clouds

as seen from a plane window, in the first rays of sunlight after ten weeks of rain, perhaps a nurse with spinach in her teeth smiling at a dying patient, who can't stop laughing. That is when God comes to call, and it is all light, and momentary wisdom, an absence of pain and a walk through simple transcendence.

The woman continues to laugh.

'Thanks, a lot, mister.'

'They're very juicy,' I say.

The red-haired woman begins to peel one of the oranges and eats it, nodding to me. She cannot stop laughing.

'Hits the spot, mister.'

I hear sirens in the distance. Suddenly I am aware that blood is spurting from the woman's arm. I take my T-shirt off and wrap it around her arm. She just keeps eating her orange, laughing, as the ambulance comes and takes her away.

Tonight the winds are high and Los Angeles is on a fire alert. I stood out on my terrace, watching the wind make waves on the pool, and saw a tree break in half in the backyard of a Twenties-style Spanish house below me.

I am on page eighty of the script and I am panicked. A door somewhere in my house is slamming back and forth from the wind. Ghosts could be flying around the room, clawing my shoulders. I need a drink. I need a loaded gun, a blowjob. I need the mambo.

A sky-blue Porsche pulls into my driveway. I can see its headlights through the dim, last moments of purple and pink sunset, shining through pollen and eucalyptus leaves swirling violently in the air.

I open my front door, peer outside, thankful for a respite. I see Joshua, sans Paula North, leaning against the Porsche.

'I thought you had a Jeep,' I shout out. Joshua looks puzzled.

'What? Oh, at the house. No, Sam, that's for the maid.'

I imagine that tiny Mexican woman in that tank. The tires are bigger than her. I guess she passes her test with flying colors. But then, she knows how to ring a bell.

'Can I come in?' Joshua shouts back at me. The wind is howling with disaster. I smile, open the door, and he runs inside. There is a beautiful quiet when the door is closed.

'Wow, Sam. Nice house. I like it. It's very Sixties.'

'I rent it.'

'Yeah, but look at this view. Bitchin'. Maybe I'll take over your lease when you leave.'

'I beg your pardon?'

'Dad said you don't like Hollywood. That you'll probably leave when the script's finished. You are leaving, aren't you?'

I nod my head. 'This is the second film I've done with Sol. See, Joshua, what would kill me is living here in between scripts, when nothing's going on.'

'And nobody's interested. I got you, man.' Joshua walks around the room. I notice a trace of seduction in his walk; a hand slightly brushing against his crotch, the half stretch, the slight flex of his arms, the way he pretends not to be keeping his eye on me.

'Hey, man, you got a beer?'

'Sorry. I got fruit juice and soda pop.'

'Oh, that's right. Dad said you were AA.'

I blanche.

'You got apple juice?'

'Sure.'

When I return from the kitchen, Joshua has pulled out and unbuttoned his shirt. He scratches his chest, sips his apple juice.

'So how's the script?' We sit down.

'Horrible.'

'I'm going to be the associate producer on this.'

'It's moving along.'

'Ah. Writer talk.'

'Let's put it this way, Joshua. Your father seems to want to turn a really tragic, violent story into another tits and slasher epic, and I find it very difficult. But I'm getting through it.'

'Somehow.'

'Exactly.'

'Look, Sam, that's what Dad does. He's no genius, but he can churn out flicks.'

'I had no idea you knew Kathi.'

'See, Sam, I didn't really *know* her. When I said she

109

was my secretary, I meant she worked the pool, with ten or twelve other girls, for extra money. I came up here to straighten that out with you. Okay?'

The wind is shaking the sliding glass doors.

'Besides,' states Joshua carefully, 'how do you know she was murdered?'

'My God, look at the body, and the surrounding evidence.'

'How do you know that was necessarily the cause of her death?' Joshua's eyes narrow.

'What do you mean?'

'What if she were already dead, from natural causes? Why would anyone want to make a movie about a plain, overweight woman who died of a stroke?'

'How do you know it was a stroke?'

Joshua begins to speak, then stops.

'What are you hiding?' I make my voice as dramatic as possible, then tap my nails on the chair arm.

'Look, I told you I didn't know this Kathi chick, and I didn't, really. I paid her to blow me in my office. I had about six different chicks, but Kathi was the best. She'd have to stop every once in a while. She had problems breathing, and see, I gotta big dick, and sometimes she'd choke a bit.'

I lick my lips unconsciously, a gesture Joshua immediately notices. No, son of producer, no, I shan't be screwing with you. I don't know what to say. Why is he telling me this? As if understanding my thoughts, Joshua smiles.

'I'm a highly sexed guy, Sam. I like shooting a load. Most of these chicks don't even have faces, you know?'

I suddenly feel ill.

'I'm going to tell you a little something, Sam.'

'Perhaps I don't want to hear.'

'Oh, but you got to, Sam.'

'And?'

'And if you ever repeat this story I'll cut your eyes out.'

Joshua says this so reasonably I shiver.

'Don't incriminate yourself with me, Joshua. I don't need to know anything.'

'Maybe this will help you with the script.' Joshua arches an eyebrow.

'Maybe it won't. Look, I'm kind of tired, Joshua.' I get up, brushing off my pants.

111

'Sit down.'

The way Joshua says this, I sit down. The door is still banging somewhere in the house. I know it must be from the back bedroom. I get up again.

'Can I close that damn door? It's driving me crazy.'

'Sure,' Joshua says, rubbing his crotch.

I understand with that one question the power structure has changed. Joshua is not in control. Someone twenty years younger than me, and in my house. I slap my forehead in the darkened bedroom. A crow is cawing on the bed, having flown in.

'Get out – shoo!' I whisper, chasing the crow out the window. I shut and bolt it in the darkness. The wind is whistling through its hinges.

'Sam, you aren't in there playing with yourself, are you?'

'No, Joshua, sorry.' I come into the living room.

'You like jackin' off, Sam?'

'C'mon, Joshua. Let's cut all this, all right?'

'I saw the way you looked at my dad. You got the hots for him, don't you?'

I say nothing. I have always prided myself on subtlety.

'There was a crow on my bed. Got in through an open window. I chased it out,' I say in a monotone. 'Some people say that's a symbol of death.'

'No, of the devil.'

'Well, anyway, I was thinking I might throw it into the script.'

'You're avoiding the subject.'

'I don't want my eyes cut out.'

Joshua grins. 'Kathi left a message for me on my desk at the studio. Said she'd fuck me all night long, for free, that night, just come over to her pad.'

'Why would she do that?' I ask quietly.

'Who the fuck knows? Maybe she wanted to try my dick up her cunt. Maybe she was in love with me, wanted to get married to a rich producer's son. Yeah, like that would ever happen.'

Coward, I think to myself. Filth.

'So I told her I'd be there, but play with her pussy a lot. Get it good and wet, and I'd come in at seven, straight from work, and I'd fuck her good and hard.'

I had thought that Kathi hadn't ever found a man. Now I knew she had fallen for a beautiful, vacant young

113

man. Perhaps in her mind she thought he would take her away from supermarket lines, late-night cable movies and the exact silence of being completely and utterly alone. Perhaps he would tell her she was beautiful, caress her breasts, give her children and a big house in the hills, the new car, the charge at Barney's. Perhaps being married, Kathi thought she would lose weight, become a beautiful woman, become powerful, be invited, called on her phone, greeted at restaurants.

'Like you fuck Paula?' I ask out loud.

'Paula won't let me fuck her. Paula lets me eat her out. That's it. I go in her bathroom and pop a load.'

I hate the way Joshua talks, and I say so.

'Just like my dad, Sam. He taught me all the tricks. Why don't you blow me right now, Sam, and if you're a good cocksucker, I'll tell Dad, and you can do him?'

'Jesus Christ.'

'I'm a Jew, Sam.'

'Do you have to tell me any more?'

'Yes. See, I get over to Kathi's, and I knock on the door. No answer. No one sees me, by the way. I open the door and say, "Kathi?" No answer. I find her in her

114

bedroom. She's wearing a really ugly bra and panty set, and she's sitting there with her hand up her cunt, dead. She had a stroke, see. Just got too excited thinking about me, I guess.'

'Of course,' I say acidly.

'I don't know what to do. I call Dad, he asks me every kind of question, then says he'll be over. Twenty minutes later, he's here with a real sharp saw and some buckets.'

'Oh my God.'

'Dad and I laughed a lot when he told me his plan. We burnt her tits a couple of times with Dad's cigar, then cut off her head, real careful, and drained the blood into pails. She was dead weight, let me tell you. Then, her hands. But Sam, you gotta remember, she was already dead. We didn't hurt or kill anyone. See? For an extra touch I put the monkey up her cunt. Then we left all kinds of strange clues. Dad had brought the pictures of The Black Dahlia. It was a neat scene, a great set-up. When it was all done, no fingerprints, clean as a whistle. Dad turned to me and said, "Joshua, *this* is how you get a movie made."'

I begin to vomit, and run from the room.

115

'What's his problem?' I hear Joshua mumble to himself.

Coming back into the living room, I sit down. I feel weak, but alert.

'So Dad's on the phone in less than a day, tying up the rights. You got to hand it to him, Sam.'

'I don't know what to say.'

'What you say is that you'll continue to do everything Dad and I tell you to do. You'll kiss our asses every fucking day you're writing this script. Finish the script. And forget Kathi Kind. She was . . .'

'A human being,' I say, tears rising to my eyes.

'A good cocksucker,' says Joshua, suddenly pensive, always innocent.

TEN

WANDA CALLS ME UP about a week after our lobster dinner.

'I'm having a girls-only lunch and I thought you should be here.'

'Thanks, Wanda.' Well, really.

'At the house, Sam, today, about one o'clock. You'll sit next to me. There'll be about fifty or sixty old broads, all of them I've known a long time in Hollywood.'

'Wanda, I'm not sure. I've got work to do on the screenplay . . .'

'You'll be here, Sam. And you're going to love it. That I can promise you.'

I quietly accept, hang up the phone. Wanda certainly keeps herself occupied with at-home entertainments, I think to myself. But then, with her freezer, why not?

The day is overtly warm, but there is a slight Pacific breeze which has textured the sky with a sapphire haziness, making chrome glitter on cars and the shadows caused by olive trees and palms seem cooler than they really are.

This is good light for diamonds, I think to myself, and the perfect day for Wanda's lunch. The hair will be stiff, and the rooms at the Encino house will feel like a Vaselined lens, and the silver and crystal will sparkle with tonality and most of all, youth.

As I pull into the driveway I see Lizabeth Scott getting out of a black Jaguar from the late Seventies and my heart skips a beat. Then Esther Williams, in an ugly blue polyester pants suit, heaves herself out of an older beige Rolls-Royce. Interesting group, I reason.

The valets that Wanda has hired are very muscular young men in tight shorts, sneakers, tight white T-shirts and baseball caps. Assumably, this is a big tip day, I think. As the line of cars slowly moves towards the front door,

I see the young men's name tags: Hi, My name is Biff,
Hi, My Name is Hank, Hi, My Name is Derek.

Actors, every one of them, of course. On my car radio,
Elvis Presley is singing 'All Shook Up'. I feel like I'm
entering some sort of new time zone, where the century
stayed put at 1960, and nothing has happened since. But
Lizabeth Scott! I remember her smoky voice, the way
her hair blew around her face in that big convertible in
Dead Reckoning with Bogart. Or Lizabeth standing under
a streetlight wearing a raincoat and looking perfectly
dangerous.

Then I suddenly know who is driving the car in front
of me. It's Mamie van Doren! Mamie van Doren! I repeat
to myself, shivering. *High School Confidential. Teacher's
Pet.* And *so* many more classics. As Mamie gets out of
her car, I notice her body is near-perfect, the breasts
large, and racked up like billiard balls, the hair blonde,
tipped, streaked, feathered. My goodness. I don't dare
guess her age.

Hi, My Name is Biff takes my car and winks.

'If you ever need auto detailing, I got my own business.
I'll make everything like new, inside, out. I call it 'Biff's

Perfect Body'. I come to your house. It's two hundred dollars.'

Biff winks again. He knows I'm driving a rental car. Every guest at this party will get the same line, the same card. Biff will pick up a gold watch and screw a couple of these old dames real hard and real good. Biff will make money. Biff will spend it. Biff will always work as a valet and a whore, making the occasional porno to make himself feel like he's *in the business*, but he never will be. And as he gets older, he will return to Des Moines, much like my story, I suppose. Just not allowed in, ever.

Biff will get married, possibly have children, spend his declining years telling tales of the stars he knew. The fact that he parked their cars will be left out. Sentences will start out, 'At Sol Seagull's cocktail party I remember how Esther Williams came up to me and told me the funniest story . . .'

And in Des Moines, Biff will be a neighborhood celebrity, someone for whom fame poorly rubbed off on, like suntan lotion on a cloudy day. The people Biff thinks are famous will fade, be replaced by younger deities that his grandchildren will know, and he will be too tired and cranky to not understand it all changes, it never stops. Hardly anyone under twenty-five knows of Lizabeth Scott or Esther Williams unless they are film buffs, and most people aren't, and Biff's world will shrink.

The day in all its dreamlike shimmer comes back to me. Biff looks at me to make sure I'm all right. I smile, take his card. He smiles, winks again, pretends to rearrange his crotch, hops in my car, and drives off into valet heaven.

'Nice house. I just love Tudor,' Mamie van Doren says brightly as we wait for the huge front doors to open.

'Me too,' I say equally as brightly.

I know I have to turn it on. The smile (thank God I brushed my teeth) has to be all-encompassing. I am going to have to be butch and bitchy at the same time, and never loosen my tie.

As the doors swing open, Wanda ushers us in.

'Darlings! Mamie, you look a dream, dear. And that *figure*. Go figure!'

Hug. Air kiss: right cheek, left cheek.

'And, Sam, you scamp. Now please come over to this side of the hall for pic-tures. We *love* pictures!'

Wanda is wearing black again, an Azzeldine Alaia mini in stretch fabric. There's not much of it. Wanda has accessorized her luncheon uniform with black tights, black high-heels, jet and diamond jewelry, and a big black rose in her hair.

We are put into groups. Because I'm the only man, I'm in the center; Mamie van Doren, Esther Williams and B-film actress and chanteuse Jacqueline Doral, and an ancient actress named Inez Cavanaugh in a wheelchair gather around me. Smile, flash.

'Where's the buffet?' Esther grumbles.

What I notice is that each woman has on red lip-stick. When the camera clicks and flashes, they drop their jaw and give big smiles that show a lot of lip, mouth, and teeth. People don't actually smile this way, but these deities do; drop your jaw, open your mouth, you show no wrinkles upstairs, around the eyes. Keep it up, keep it bright, you're having the time of your life. Keep the lipstick red. Later, when I see the snapshots, I look morose with my sincere smile, next to these great pearl and red butterflies floating around me.

'Now, one more shot,' Wanda huffs. 'Shelley, get over here.'

'Oh, do I have to? I'm hungry.' Miss Shelley Winters ambles up next to me. I begin to sweat.

'Wow. It's really you.' I could slap myself.

'Uh. Uh.'

Smile. Flash. Move on. To the bar and buffet. There are eight tables for six each, with gold lamé tablecloths and their own miniature working fountains as center-pieces, and surprisingly, it is pretty in this hazy Encino sun. A blind Chinese man is playing a baby grand piano, located frighteningly close to the deep end of Wanda's Romanesque-Tudor-Southwestern pool. Wanda has used placecards with small photographs of naked men attached.

'For the girls,' Wanda says from behind me.

'What's with all this gold lamé? All your plates and glasses are going to slip and slide,' says Grace Montgomery-Steinlitz, famous producer's wife. Grace has renewed my faith in the afternoon. Her hair is so stiff it must cause pain.

123

'The gold lamé had been carefully taped, Grace. Now go and enjoy yourself,' Wanda says huskily, then turns to me.

'Grace really thinks she's somebody important. Big producer's wife. Well, ever since Sam Steinlitz's colostomy they haven't made a picture. And *that's* been twenty years, Sam.'

'So what you're telling me, Wanda, is this isn't a party where I'm going to get inside information on Michael Eisner and Barry Diller, or new Hollywood contracts on the Internet. What I *am* going to find out about is Sam Steinlitz's colostomy.'

'I said it was old broads, Sam. You came.'

'You ordered me to come.'

'So I did. They still are powerful women, Sam. They're still movie stars.'

'Once a star, always a star?'

'Exactly. So be nice, tough guy. Otherwise I'll have Sol fire you. Writers are a dime a dozen. I like you because you're a queen, Sam, so be a queen today at lunch. *Entertain* these ladies.'

124   I am stunned. No one in my life has ever spoken to

me this way, with such rapid venom. I thought Wanda was my friend. As if sensing what I'm thinking, Wanda flashes me a dazzling smile.

'Look, Sam, I didn't mean to get testy, but you started it. I like you a lot, Sam. You're a kick in the behind. I hope you will consider me your friend. We're a rough group of broads, Sam. We've been there, and none of these old girls takes guff from anyone. That's why we're still here.'

'March on, glittering waxworks. I can smell the embalming fluid, Wanda.'

'Be nice, Sam.'

'Okay.' It seems suddenly like the right thing to do. Why fight? Have a nice lunch, discuss the mythic proportions of Sylvia Plath's poetry with Shelley Winters, then leave. And don't return.

I am seated next to Wanda, with Jacqueline Doral on my other side. Opposite are more B-goddesses from the Fifties; JoAnn Lee, the tempestuous black-haired star of such Republic classics as *Volcano Venus*, *Return to Monterrey*, and *Bomba Goes To Siam*. I am forewarned that Miss Lee has a drinking problem. Also Paige Russell, *Collier's* cover girl and Fifties debutante, and Anita Arnold, who, along with Jacqueline Doral, made all those smoky 'When Sunny Gets Blue' types of records in the early Sixties. The queens of smoke, martinis, spike heels and hi-fis.

'Hello, Miss Lee, I'm Samuel Johnson. I'm working with Wanda's husband, Sol, on his new picture.'

'Call me JoAnn.' Miss Lee raises her double margarita and takes a good deep gulp. Her eyes glaze over, her smile sets.

'JoAnn. I remember *Volcano Venus*, when you were being prepared to be thrown into that volcano. All those white flowers!'

There are nods around the table, a hopeful murmur of civilized conversation.

Miss Lee's hair, which is still black and long and curly, is actually a wig, and I realize it is slightly askew, as though she's spent her life walking through crooked rooms, fun-house rooms. Miss Lee raises her margarita glass one more time to her lips, downs the remainder, licks the salt off the rim, purses her lips from the sudden rush of acid.

'Oh no,' Wanda sighs under her breath.

'Get me another one.' Miss Lee snaps her fingers at one of the catering staff. Wanda pulls the young man and I hear her whisper, 'No tequila this time.' Miss Lee is oblivious. She raises one eyebrow and focuses all her attention on me.

'What's your name again?'

'Samuel.'

'Well, Sam, you look like you got a big juicy cock. Why don't you show it to us, right now? Here at the table?'

'Jo-Ann . . .' Jacqueline Doral taps her nails on the gold lamé and tries to interrupt, but Miss Lee is on a roll.

'You know, Sam, I'd like you to fuck me with that big cock of yours. We can go upstairs. What do you say?'

'I say I think all you have to do is call one of Wanda's parking valets.'

Wanda rolls her eyes. I look over to Miss Lee and she has closed hers, a crooked smile on her lips. She is sitting up perfectly still. I would assume, at this moment, that she is a very proper, quiet blind woman.

'Out like a light. She'll be back in twenty minutes, sober as a judge,' Wanda says quietly. 'Oh, look. Here comes the main course. I hope you like scallops and Caesar salad.'

Drinks all around the table, except for me and Miss Lee, the two drunks. The girls are loosening up. As Miss Lee stays in her state of Mexican rigor mortis, tequila pulsing through her like river water at a power plant, I am asked a question by Paige Russell.

'So, is it big?'

Titters around the table.

'Yes,' I say noncommittally.

More titters. I realize I am the *object* of this table. The *man*. (All penises in Hollywood are big; one always insists this is the biggest cock in town.) Whether or not I prefer showing my big penis to another man instead of a woman is not of import at this table.

'God, I remember Bogie's,' Jacqueline whispers to the table.

'And what about John Ireland and Leif Erickson? And Forrest Tucker? Those men were *gifted*,' Anita Arnold says quietly. 'I dated all three of them way back when.'

'It's amazing you can still walk,' Wanda says archly.

More titters around the table.

'What about Chaplin?' I ask.

All four women that are still coherent nod their heads.

'Of course.'

'Common knowledge.'

'Charlie couldn't keep it in his pants.'

'Even when he was old . . .'

'Tallulah used to get on the phone and rave about John Emery, one of her husbands. Said it was *monumental*,' states Jacqueline Doral.

'What about Don Johnson? I hear it's like a baseball bat!' I shriek accidentally, giving my gayness a new, middle-aged light.

Silence.

Paige Russell lights a Camel cigarette. 'Isn't he that TV actor who married Tippi Hedren's daughter?'

'Yes, he's a big star.' Silence. Confusion.

'How is Tippi, Wanda? You both still speaking?' Anita Arnold asks.

'Tippi's a doll. I don't like all those lions and tigers she keeps. Their fur makes me sneeze. She loves them, though.

'Let's get back to Sam. How would you rate yourself on a scale of . . .'

'Enough about my penis, ladies. Let's talk about careers.' See, Wanda, I can be a sport, too.

Before a frost has a chance to settle in at the table, Trudy Chevalier-Weinberg, a birdlike little woman in a yellow St John cotton suit (and a good friend of Grace Montgomery-Steinlitz) is mad and letting Wanda know it.

'I had to use the powder room. I hadn't even touched my chicken, and I came back and Shelley Winters has taken all the food off my plate and literally dumped it on hers. No apologies, nothing. She looks up at me and says, "Well, honey, you weren't eating your food," and I say, "Shelley, they just sat it down in front of me!" Two minutes in the powder room. For God's sake! Wanda, I don't see how you can have that woman at a lunch.'

Wanda clasps Trudy's hand, signals a waiter and arranges a new plate of food for her. When Mrs Chevalier-Weinberg takes her leave, Wanda turns and says to the table, 'I invite Shelley because she takes *every-thing* home. There's no clean-up.'

130

More titters around the table.

'Talking about career, Sam,' Paige Russell says casually, 'they've written a book about my life. There's talk of a film.'

'What did you think of Eric Roots' book on poor dear Lana?' Jacqueline Doral says angrily.

'Terrible. But then what do you expect from a *hairdresser*? You know the type.' Paige Russell sniffs.

Anita Arnold looks up brightly.

'They're releasing all my old recordings as a CD series.'

'Like *Jazz For Lonely Nights*, and *Hi-Fi Heaven*?' I ask eagerly. My first true thoughts of the possibility of serious drag came from those LP covers, with Anita Arnold stretched out in silver capri pants and glittery spike heels on top of a grand piano, a stem glass with a cherry in her hand, ready for pain and heartbreak in that delicious cocktail lounge light.

'God, you remember those. They were actually pretty good, weren't they?'

'The best.' This is good news to me. No colostomies, big penises, or Shelley Winters. Just a small return to glory.

'They want me to do a series of concerts on these cruise ships. The money's good, full orchestra, a costume budget. I just don't know.'

'Why?' I ask.

'Well, they're for senior citizens, these cruises. I don't know, I hear they're good audiences, but I want to sing in front of regular audiences in regular venues. I mean, I'm *not* that old.'

Suddenly, from around the table there is a loud rush of recognition.

'Of course you're not.'

'Being told that . . . I'd sue.'

'You don't look a day over forty.'

'Who needs to work a cruise? You've got tons of money, Anita.'

It is in Anita Arnold's eyes that I understand who we are. I, the occasional man, the divertissement, and these girls who will stay as perfect as possible for longer than reason. In Anita's gaze there is complete fear, the blood pop of a dying sparrow's eyes. She is the only woman at this table with any real talent, the kind people remember, and enjoy, and Anita Arnold doesn't want to age. She is sixty-five years old and wears tight white jeans with a gold lamé belt, high heels and a Gap stretch mock turtleneck. Her hair is frizzed into a cascade of curls and she has had six husbands.

It's as if the mention of age brings dark clouds in, that the rhythm and flow of the deities survives on everything but the present, and its obvious, squalid truths.

I look at Jacqueline Doral, who piles on the diamonds, cinching in her waist too tight. Or Paige Russell, with her exaggerated eyebrows, those Liz Taylor eyebrows that looked good in 1965, and of course, Wanda, my new favorite enemy, my film noir housewife, and her practiced smirk.

The blind Chinese man continues to play requests like 'Misty' or 'The Theme From Pocahontas' as dessert is served. Our table lapses into a lazy luxury, the spin being we are all rich and young until we die, we are in Holly-wood, we *matter*, we are *desired*.

JoAnn Lee opens her eyes and accidentally knocks over a glass of mineral water.

'Jesus, I'm hungry. When's lunch?'

JoAnn Lee stares at me, and flashes a red butterfly smile.

'You're a nice-looking man. Are you a friend of Wanda's? What's your name?'

JoAnn Lee begins to tackle her scallops and Caesar salad. Wanda giggles.

'You know, Wanda's a great, great hostess. Everyone thinks so. Oh look, a margarita. Wanda, I told you I wasn't drinking margaritas today. Waiter, I'll have a Bombay martini please.'

ELEVEN

I AM DOING WELL with the script, but it is a slow go. The only way I can see it, the way Sol wants it, is to write it fresh, in that Kathi Kind did not exist, and I can remember her only when I don't write. The new 'movie' Kathi Kind is thirty-four with a great figure, soft blonde hair and plenty of it, a great, attractive face, just like Paula North, of course.

This Kathi Kind gets murdered at the beginning of the picture, hack, hack, hands and head, while she's taking a long, steamy cliché shower. Then, in flashbacks, we find out Kathi worked as a topless dancer in an upscale night club, 'The Furry Kitten' on LaCienega, in order to pay her way through college, where she is studying to be a special education teacher, as she wants to teach the deaf, and sits in on a Sunday school class for pre-school deaf children. I wrote a great scene where Kathi signs the story of Abraham to a small group of incredibly cute deaf children who adore her, of course.

Kathi Kind lives alone up in the hills in a spacious, steel and glass house (obviously she must make a great deal in tips, as a home like this in Los Angeles runs at about seven hundred thousand dollars). In the evenings she doesn't work, Kathi sips coffee from a Smiley mug and, with pencil behind ear, tries to figure out all the new software on her computer.

Kathi, of course, has several buxom, and kind, stripper girlfriends with hearts of gold, and of course, they are all going to college, and this is the *only* work they can find. There's Louella, the Afro-American spitfire, who's studying to be a doctor of psychology and has a little son, Rodney; and Trish, the Girl Most Likely To, who insists she's leaving as soon as she gets her interior design diploma. Sol really likes this. The girls all celebrate birthdays together and wear perky jeans outfits.

But Kathi's best friend is Maria, who got her in at the Sunday school for the deaf. Maria is an attractive, and of course, busty, Hispanic woman who is tough but kind, and of course, adores Kathi Kind. Oh God. Everyone loves Kathi.

Now *all* the stripper babes get chopped up, Sol writes to me in a memo, but Maria has to survive. Somebody's got to survive. And make sure the victims have no clothes on. I want to see pussy. Make sure their breasts shake.

Yes, Sol. No, Sol. Of course, Sol.

Kathi, Louella and Trish are of course being stalked by a horrible drooling psycho (we're hoping for John Glover) whom Maria finally shoots in guess what? An abandoned warehouse. Maria shoots El Psycho Hombre with a sawed-off shotgun and blows most of his head off, which winds up at the bottom of an empty grain silo.

I hate warehouse endings. Nine out of ten movies have a climax in a warehouse and it's always the same thing, the steel stairs, the pistol that gets dropped and kicked away, the running around between cardboard boxes. Jesus.

Yes, Sol notes, but we have a *Hispanic* woman who saves the day. Oh, and Sam, make sure at some point her shirt gets ripped and we can see her tits.

Will do, Sol, no problem. Yes, Sol, I can see how *current*, how *Nineties* this ending can be. What else, Sol? Well, I'm sure I could figure out a way to see one of her nipples, at least. But I don't know. What? You've decided you want her topless at the end, her tits shaking as she fires away with the big sawed-off shotgun? You may have an insurance with that one, Sol. Powder burns. I see, well, it's an idea I'm sure we can knock around tomorrow at lunch.

TWELVE

SOL WON'T TAKE WANDA out for lunch or dinner, but here we are, having a beautiful meal at Morton's, a place I wouldn't normally think of Sol at. The Hillcrest Country Club, yes, or the Bistro Garden, or Valentino. But Morton's is too high-end for Sol.

He keeps waving over to David Geffen's table as though he knows him, then quickly glances around the room to see if anyone caught his wave. Of course, several people did. Smiles flash. Sol nods his head, feels secure, orders a double Scotch. No one knows Sol here. And no one cares.

'Great place, Sam. Just like old times.'

'You know, this lamb chop doesn't compete with the ones Hiro was chopping in your kitchen.'

'Wanda really likes that little rice paddy.'

'Hmmm.'

'You know why I don't take Wanda out, don't you, Sam?'

'No. It does seem a bit odd.'

'She makes me look old.'

'No she doesn't,' I say quickly. Get over yourself, Sol Seagull. You're in your sixties with white hair and a hearing aid.

'Truthfully? Okay, Sam, I'll tell you. I keep Wanda around the house because I'm scared she's gonna leave me.'

'What?'

'See Sam, Wanda likes men. She likes them a lot. One time we went to New York together and she disappeared for three days with the head doorman of the Waldorf-Astoria. I told her I had grounds to divorce her then and she said if I even tried she'd cut off my balls and fry them for breakfast, and Sam, I believe her.'

'Don't forget, Sol, California is a community property state.'

'Exactly. So let her stay home. She can do whatever the hell she wants, as long as she doesn't get wild on the outside and make me look like a fool.'

'Does Wanda agree?'

Sol's face turns dark, and menacing.

'Wanda *has* to agree.'

Sol's cellular phone rings. He takes it, pressing it up to his good ear.

'Hiya, Josh. Uh-huh. Well shit, kid, why didn't you call sooner? We'll be right over.' Sol puts down his phone.

'Just what I don't need. Paula North is trying to jump out her apartment window.'

'Can't Joshua keep her in?'

'You don't know my son too well, Sam. He's a good-lookin', bright kid, but he's a coward.'

We are in Sol's Jaguar, racing down Beverly Boulevard towards Park La Brea, where Paula has an apartment. Pulling into the intricate maze of driveways and parking lots, Sol stops the car.

'There she is. Goddamit. Goddamit.'

Paula is sitting, with her feet dangling, in the window casement of her tenth-floor apartment. She is wearing a motorcycle jacket and her best underwear, a lacy cream-toned French brassière and matching panties. She has put on a glamorous pair of high-heeled, lizard-skin sandals. I assume this decision was made when Paula realized if she does kill herself, she will want to be remembered as having great legs, and those sandals give a great line and curve. You write the show when you kill yourself.

Sol gets out of the Jag and motions me to follow. Walking hurriedly towards Paula's building, I notice how the sky is an evil blue, like Japanese china from the Second World War. The Hollywood Hills to our left seem fuzzy with auto exhaust and the steam of sprinklers. I figure that Paula is ninety feet from the ground, two miles from those Hollywood Hills, fifteen feet from her front door, and about fifteen feet from her bed.

It was in her bed, last night, that Paula tried to end her beautiful aimlessness with a full bottle of Desipramine, but wound up having diarrhea and some pretty intense vomiting. She did lose almost seven pounds, something she's wanted for a long time.

Sol races into the building. I stand, looking up for just a moment. Paula's hair is floating softly in the Santa Ana winds, which have chapped her lips. She looks straight down and sees me and three teenage boys staring up at her. They are leering, smiling, wiping their noses. Holding on to one part of the window, Paula slides her panties off and throws them down to the boys. They yell and begin to run around like dogs. Then, taking the side of the other window for support, she unhooks her brassière and throws it down as well.

She claps her legs and feet together like a child on a swing, half in, half out, and I wonder if someone has bothered to call 911, or bothered even to lift a receiver.

Paula almost loses her balance as she takes off her leather jacket and throws it down. One of the boys next to me is giggling, and pulls down his pants and waves his penis at her. It must look quite forlorn from the tenth floor, I think. Paula begins to laugh.

All three teenage boys begin motioning for her to jump, like this is a game. One boy keeps shouting up that he's her friend, that he'll catch her. Don't, Paula, I whisper, he's the devil, a white mamba, a scorpion in tennis shoes.

143

Then I see a thick arm and hand, Sol's to be exact, pull Paula in roughly and close the window. I hurry inside, up to the tenth floor, where I can hear the sound of breaking furniture.

As I open the door, I see Joshua sitting on a sofa in his underwear, crying. Sol has Paula by the hair.

'You stupid, junkie cunt!'

Sol punches Paula in the stomach so hard she doubles over, falling on to a small English mahogany side-table. He grabs her by her hair again, opening her mouth with three fingers and forcing them down her throat until she begins to vomit. Sol wipes his hand with a handkerchief and checks on Paula, crossing his arms.

'See, Sam, in case the cops *do* come, and they won't, we're going to get all that dope out of her stomach now.'

When Paula is finished, she looks up at Sol first, then me. I have a terror. A small terror, a hallucination that lasts only long enough for me to touch my rapidly beating heart. I see Kathi Kind in Paula's vomit-covered face. Kathi Kind says, gee, Sam, don't worry about all this. I'm still going to be somebody special. These people are filth, Samuel, but they're everywhere, like locusts in Egypt, you just can't get rid of them until they've devoured their fair share. Nothing more to be done, Samuel, nothing more to be done.

'What are you looking at?' Paula North says to me quietly. She's naked, doesn't seem to be aware of it.

'You. You're a fucking picture, Paula,' Sol interrupts, going into the bathroom and getting a towel and a robe. Back in the living room, Sol throws the towel and robe at Paula.

'Clean your mess up, Paula, and then fix us some coffee.'

'I don't know if I can walk.'

'You can walk. And shut the fuck up with the crying, Joshua. You're my son, not some fucking pansy.'

Joshua wipes his eyes, then turns to me.

'We were both pretty high, see, but I didn't think Paula would try anything crazy. She told me if I touched her she'd jump, so I called Dad. Dad always knows what to do.'

Sol collapses into a chair, exhausted.

'Oh, fuck you, you little moron.'

Paula shakily gets up, holding a sopping towel, and

slowly, jerkily makes her way towards the kitchen.

'Don't forget cream and sugar.'

'Yes, Sol,' Paula says, beaten.

'Sol?'

'Yes, Sam?'

'Why do you treat women this way?'

'What?'

'Like Paula, just now – and now we're going to sit down and have *coffee*?'

'Let me explain, Sam. I just did Paula a favor. I just gave her a Brooklyn stomach pump. No hospital, no press. Paula's a cheap piece of shit, but right now she's a movie star, and I protect my interests, but by protecting mine I'm also protecting hers. Paula North'll wind up a rich woman someday, and she'll thank me for it. Don't forget, Sam, I pulled her in. I saved her life.'

I think of those teenage boys, like little coyotes, still waiting for the window to reopen. I get up and look down at the parking lot. The one boy has pulled his pants up now, and all three are on their backs, kicking their legs and arms and staring up at the sky, laughing hysterically. One boy has Paula's bra on his face; another is wearing

146

her panties as a shower cap, and is pretending to scrub himself. The boy who had his pants down is wearing Paula's black motorcycle jacket and is lewdly rubbing his crotch.

What a day, the three of them think. A naked lady day.

THIRTEEN

WANDA OPENS THE FRONT door. She is wearing a silver and black peignoir to the floor, something I have always wanted to see a woman wear, but I didn't think they existed outside of Barbara Stanwyck films.

'You'd better come in, Sam.'

Her voice is fearful, cagey.

'Let's go someplace where Sol . . . Let's go into the kitchen.'

I sit down on the black suede sofa. Wanda sits down next to me, a glass of Glenlivet in hand, and stares at me.

'I think Sol is going to have you killed, Sam.'

'What?'

'Joshua and Sol are upstairs right now, fighting like you wouldn't believe. What did Joshua tell you? Are Sol and Joshua up to something bad?'

Wanda's eyebrows jump.

'Actually, no, Wanda, nothing I know about.'

'You're lying. All men in Hollywood lie. You and my husband have a secret. And you aren't going to tell me anything.' Wanda stares directly into my eyes, waiting for a response. I say nothing.

'Well, I'm going to help you, little man, and you'd better listen to me, and listen good. In the last thirty years Sol has bumped three or four people off, at least that I know of, and I keep my mouth shut. I don't see anything. I don't know anything. But I've learnt how to collect.'

'Why do you think he's after me? We've been good friends.'

'Sam, Sol's not your friend. He's your employer. Oh, I saw the way you looked at the old bastard. You'd hop in the sack with him if you could. He's old and he's ugly, but man is he rich.'

I feel myself becoming angry. Am I that transparent? Am I a whore?

'That's beyond the point, because as far as I know my husband isn't a fag. But you found out something last night. My son told you something he won't even tell me. And my husband has hit the roof, and will probably take out a contract on you in the next hour. Now what is it?'

I shrug my shoulders.

'You're a fool.'

'Maybe.'

'Follow me, we're going to listen in at the door of Sol's study. You're going to have to be very quiet, Sam. I'll be right there with you.'

Behind the Seagull study door, there is shouting. I hear Joshua's voice.

'I figured he'd be like, bound to us. That we'd get him cheaper next time, the way you do it, when you hire private detectives to get dirt on –'

'You idiot! You get dirt on *him*, not on *us*. Idiot! We could be put away for a long time; lose our house, the movies, everything. Idiot!'

'Sorry, Dad.' Joshua's voice sounds casual. I suddenly

hear the sound of somebody being punched. I motion to Wanda that we need to flee for the moment. Soon we are back in the black marble kitchen.

Wanda takes my hand and holds it, a gesture I find strangely horrifying.

'Now listen to me, Sam. Don't say anything. Good. Have you finished the script?'

I nod my head. The last three minutes could still use a rewrite . . .

'Okay. It's Saturday evening, so the banks are closed, and won't be open again till Monday at nine. Sam, Sol is going to offer you the rest of your fee in cash. How much does he owe you?'

'Eighty thousand dollars.;

'If I know Sol, he'll give you eighty thousand dollars in cash tonight in a manila envelope, and congratulate you on a job well done. He'll put the hit on you tonight, for either Sunday night or Monday morning. The hit man will take his fee out of the cash in your envelope and return the rest to Sol as proof. No banks, no checks, clean as a whistle.'

'No banks, no checks,' I repeat numbly to myself.

'Keep listening. You're going to have to clear out fast,

152

and I mean fast, Sam. Don't tell Sol where you're going. Lie. If you don't, you're dead. I figure Sol will get our hit man, Bill, a nice guy if there ever was one, wife and two kids in high school, a house in Torrance. Bill's slow, but he's discreet. He won't show up till late Sunday night, when he thinks you'll be asleep, so you're going to have to clear out by dusk. Got it?'

I nod my head.

'I'm trying to help you, Sam. You were always kind of fun. Now generally Bill charges about twenty thousand a hit, I know 'cause I eavesdropped on one of Sol's conversations about four years ago. My suggestion is this: leave twenty thousand in cash on the counter in your kitchen. See, someone like Bill gets paid either way. He'll explain to Sol he doesn't know where you are, that you disappeared, but he got paid, his mouth is shut. You *always* pay the hit man, Sam. They'll talk.'

I shake my head in disbelief.

'It's all cash, sweetie. If you declared it and paid taxes, that twenty thousand dollars would go to the IRS, anyway. And you're on a plane, sixty thousand dollars in your pocket.

153

'Sort of like leaving milk and cookies for Santa,' I say uneasily.

'Sol won't follow you once you're on your plane, Sam. Sol never leaves Hollywood. God knows we haven't been on a vacation in forty years. I always wanted to see Paris. Just don't tell Sol anything else about you, ever.'

The house seems suddenly silent. Wanda's miniature maid arrives, all four feet of her, holding a large bag of groceries, which I help her with.

'Gracious, *señor*.' She looks up and makes a sign of the cross, scurrying away from me.

'Go and knock on Sol's door, Sam. Get it over with, see if I'm right, and then get the hell out. Don't say I never did you a favor.' Wanda manages a weak smile, turning at once to the tiny woman.

'Today, *señorita*, you're going to learn how to pickle mackerel. You *comprende*? Pickle mackerel.'

I am numb, completely alone. I knock on Sol's door.

'It's open.'

Joshua is sitting on a red leather couch next to Sol's desk, nursing a black eye. The Venetian blinds on Sol's windows are half open, creating bright lines of light throughout the room.

'Hi, Joshua,' I say pleasantly.

'Hey, Sam.'

Sol gets up, shakes my hand.

'So, Sam, looks like this script is *el finito*. You're a real pro, Sam. I'm very pleased.'

'Thanks, Sol.'

'By the way, I was very upset about what Josh said to you last night. None of it's true. See, Joshua is a real kidder. When he was a kid he used to tell the weirdest fucking stories, none of them true. He's a liar.'

'Well, Sol, I didn't really think . . .'

'Of course, Sam, you're a gentleman.'

'Thanks, Sol.'

'I've got a big surprise for you, Sam.' Sol puts his glasses on and shifts through several contracts on his desk.

'Ah, here we are.' Sol brings out a large alligator case, not really a briefcase – bigger, squarer. He snaps it open. Inside must be about two or three million dollars. Sol counts out four bundles and puts them into a large manila envelope.

155

'There you go, Sam. Paid in cash. And let me tell you, thanks again for a job *well* done. I couldn't have done it without you, kid. Eighty thousand dollars, Sam. We're through, I believe. You go have a good time.'

Sol shakes my hand and offers a polite, strange kiss on my cheek.

'I like you a lot, Sam.'

'I like you, too, Sol.'

'See ya.'

'See ya.'

'I'll call you tomorrow, just for a chat.'

'Sure, Sol.'

As I close the door behind me I try to make my way through this house, keeping my eyes closed, feeling my way like the suddenly blinded. Kathi Kind is behind me, pushing me towards Sol and Wanda Seagull's front door. Kathi is whispering, laughing, telling me I'm a nice guy, but she doesn't need me anymore, and she never really did.

I open the huge, carved doors and walk outside towards my car. No one has seen me out, or waved goodbye, even

half-heartedly.

FOURTEEN

THERE ARE PEOPLE WHO walk on smoking coals, pass their hand through fire and emerge smiling, undamaged, as though a great mystery of concentration is theirs for the asking. These people are smart enough to know they won't be able to walk on burning carbon all their lives; but they will pass through fire a few times, just for the hell of it, just to show the world they could, and retire before they become a statistic.

It is Sunday. I am packing my bags. I am running a comb through my hair, disconnecting the telephone.

When I spoke to Sol today I was cheerful, and so was

he. I told him that with my Hollywood money I would be taking a long sojourn in Europe, perhaps Greece, and that I wanted to be left completely alone to write the novel I had always wanted to write.

Sol seemed pleased at my quiet decision, then asked me if there was a place I could be contacted. Pleasantly, I told him no, though I would receive correspondence through my agent, I will just be on the move so much. Travelling, you know. Sol chuckled.

'We'll miss you at the première,' he said gruffly.

'I know you've got a hit,' I managed weakly.

Silence.

'So tell me, Sam, what's this book going to be about?'

I explained to Sol it would be a coming-of-age story of a young, Tom Sawyer type in a sleepy Southern town. Again, Sol seemed pleased. I, of course, lied.

'Let me buy the rights, Sam. Let me buy them now.'

'I don't think so, Sol. Let me write it first.'

'Fair enough. You know, Sam, you're the only writer I ever liked working with. You're a real smart guy.'

'Thanks, Sol.'

'We'll work together again, Sam. Maybe a comedy.

Something without all this blood and guts. Something where you and I could have some fun, some laughs.'

'Sure, Sol. Soon.'

'You take it easy, Sam.'

'You too, Sol. Give my best to Wanda.'

'Will so.'

End of conversation.

I have not told Sol I am actually taking a plane to Mexico City in an hour, and then another to Panama City, where I have rented a penthouse apartment in a condominium complex filled with ex-dictators, the ex-wives of ex-dictators, and others who know too much.

My Hollywood money will last for a while. I have put my cottage in White Plains, New York up for sale, via the Internet, and I will probably never return. I suddenly think of Kathi Kind's sister, Sue Ellen, and wonder how her Hollywood money went. It'll be money to keep me invisible, a dead commodity, money that I'll spend too fast, money that will kill me.

In the steam of Panama, under palms with actual coco-nuts and young boys with milk chocolate skin, I shall write down everything I know, change the names, sell it in two or three years for an enormous sum. I shall put on weight, begin to really look middle-aged, start drinking again. This is how you vanish, I think. This is how you leave.

There is where I am going today. I am packing so fast I barely know what I'm doing, in a Los Angeles that crawls like a wolf spider through my bones, an incense of still living bodies, unaware of themselves. I have lived here long enough. I have pandered to myself with forbidden walks through the opiates, through streets burnt by flowers the color of storms. And I have never stopped to wipe it off.

The palms around my box on Mulholland Drive are blooming, and the heavy floss of this pollen is drifting through the air like plankton. I zip up my suitcase and turn on the radio. Sadé is singing 'Smooth Operator'. It is an old song, but it's played every day in Hollywood.

I am going to a place where I cannot speak the language, so I know I will feel at home. I returned my rental car last night, counted the keys to the house, the china, the crystal, the bed linens. Everything is as it was. Even my scent has disappeared. I now have to wait for a taxi to take me to LAX. The phone will disconnect automatically in the morning. Someone will buy a postcard of Grauman's Chinese Theatre, of the Santa Monica Pier, and on each card a happy cartoon of a blazing, smiling sun, wearing sunglasses, will be beneficent and welcoming in the corner of the card.

The air is thick and honeyed and full of helicopters, radios, orange blossoms and newly applied manure. I shiver. I am suddenly cold.

It is possible to rise from ash and debris. The first step is water, a damp rag, a comb. The next step is escape. You bathe yourself like a child. The water is warm, your heart is cold. You look around and say to yourself, I've never been here, this doesn't exist.

You mask the smell of cinder and black wood on your arms, and chance upon your reflection again. Your breath is cluttered, unsure, lacking music. It is the same twitch of gypsy moths, ambivalent to distance, focused on light.

There is no new face for you yet; only a color you move to, changing each hour with the precision of birth. You will vanish.

This is the religion of becoming someone else, of rising

with wings of fire. Forget your family. Forget your friends. They no longer exist. Forget your lovers. They love someone else and will no longer recognize you.

The only thing you have is your skin. Your hide, the branded fur. That you can mold. It stretches in your hand and obeys.

Think of points of departure. Think of roads cutting mountains the color of mink, valleys that blink with women's eyes. Grab everything. Give nothing away.

Soon you will be someone invisible, in the invisible heat of an invisible situation, a geography visited on a dare. Look into men's bellies to see what they've eaten. Look up to the moon. Rub your hand on a strange wall. The dust of a new life will cover your palm.

It is then, and only then, you will become someone else, the next step, the purifier, the rush of fast forward, the pure movie star, still perfect in the answer print, never cauterized by the seasons.

Do not blink, or it will go away, and you will lose yourself for ever.

This is what I am thinking at the edge of the world, on the top of a mountain waiting for a taxi to hell, where violence will come to an empty house, and it is the only place, and only at this moment, that I can peer into the still red embers of a charred fire to see where I've been.

EPIL●GUE

AFTER I LEAVE, TERRIFIED for my life, Wanda will arrive at
my rental house at midnight, dressed in tight black bicycle
pants, black Charles Jourdan high heels, a black
turtleneck like Anne Francis used to wear on *Honey West*,
and a black beret.

The house will be dark, but instead of using a flashlight,
as her outfit certainly dictates, Wanda will turn the lights
on, light a cigarette and walk towards my kitchen, the
place I never cooked or ate in anyway.

She will see a manila envelope and hurriedly open
it. Inside will be Monopoly play money, shredded

newspapers, a crisp twenty dollar bill that's real, and a note from me:

'Sorry, Wanda, but I've written a scene just like this two years ago, for a European film. Maybe next time. I must say, you gave it a good shot.'

Wanda crumples up the note, throws it on the floor, stubs her cigarette on the granite counter.

'Damn.' She takes a small piece of tobacco off her tongue and flicks it at the wall.

'Damn.'